SEETHER'S
SIMPLE PLAN
War Angels MC

Table of Contents

Prologue
Seether
Afghanistan, 4 Years ago

"Sir we have an all clear." I said into my com, not shifting my gaze from the scope of my sniper rifle. "There is one woman in the hut and she is uncovered sir, no burka."

"10-4 Morgan." My superior officer said in my ear. I lay in my position for another five minutes, not hearing or seeing anything. My breathing was calm and relaxed and my heart beat was slow and steady. Then from the corner of my eye some billowing dust caught my eye.

"Sir we've got some movement 30 clicks to the north. Too much dust to be a camel sir looks to be a fast moving vehicle."

"Hold tight Morgan, report back."

"Yes sir." I waited a few more minutes as the truck came closer to our position. "Sir there appears to be five tangos in the truck; four with visible fire power, sir the driver is unknown."

"10-4 Morgan, hold your position and your fire."

"Yes sir." I waited and watched as the truck pulled up to the hut and one of the men got out and went inside. The woman was obviously frightened and tried frantically to cover her head and face in front of this strange man. Instead he ripped the scarf away from her and threw it to the dirt floor.

"Sir this situation is about to go sideways." I reported, watching in horror as the man threw the woman to the floor with her scarf and started pulling at her clothes.

"Hold your fire Sergeant; we cannot give away our position."

"Sir he's raping her sir," I rasped out. "Sir?"

"Hold Sergeant!"

I stayed in position, watching the terror in front of me as each of the five men in the truck went into the house and each raped the woman. By the time the last man was finally finished the woman had stopped fighting. I thought she was dead until she slowly blinked and I saw a tear streak down her cheek and drip off her nose. I could have sworn she was staring right at me and she knew I was there and had done nothing.

"They're done sir." I reported, trying to keep the sound of my own agonized tears out of my voice. I don't think I succeeded and I stopped caring as the men climbed back into the truck and drove away laughing. "All clear sir."

I pulled away from my scope slightly to wipe the tears from my eyes that made my vision blurry. By the time I looked back to the little hut it had exploded in a flash so bright I was seeing stars and the screams of my troupe dying over the radio was all I heard.

Present Day
Grace-Lynn

"Please Gracie, step into my office." Little D said, smiling nastily. I hated it when he called me Gracie, my name is Grace-Lynn.

"What do you need D?" I asked walking through the door and stopping when it was slammed behind me. I turned to see two of D's guys standing there sneering at me. "What's going on D?"

"It would seem Gracie that you have outlived your usefulness." D replied, stepping out from behind his desk.

"What-?" before I could get it all out a meaty hard fist connected with my cheek that sent me slumping to the floor.

I suppose I should be grateful after the first few kicks one of the guys kicked me in the head and I passed out. So I missed most of the beating. I could feel the effects though.

Unfortunately I woke up just as D was ripping my pants down my legs and I was awake while he raped me. I fought him as hard as I could, screaming and thrashing but I still felt him shove himself into me. I thought the pain from him beating me was bad, but the sharp tearing deep inside me was far worse.

I finally cried and fought enough that he knocked me out again and the next thing I remember was Edith trying to clean me up, sweet awesome amazing Edith.

Merry Christmas to me.

CHAPTER 1

Boxing Day
Grace-Lynn

When I woke up I could tell I wasn't alone in the room. What or where the room was I didn't know. I did know that there was the comfortable sound of computer terminals humming around me. Was I at home? No, home didn't have that warm masculine scent.

I cracked my eyes open just slightly and saw a man sitting at a wall of computer monitors with his back to me. He was huge, I could tell that even though he was sitting and he had thick sandy blond hair. I may have gasped slightly at the sight because he froze but he didn't turn.

When he moved like I thought he might turn I closed my eyes again. I counted to ten and then opened them the tiniest slit. I should've counted to one hundred. The guy at the computers had turned around and was now staring at me. Caught I opened my eyes all the way and blinked at him then tried to scoot to the far side of the bed.

"It's okay Pixie." He said, his voice was deep and raspy and he looked like he was exhausted, his dark green eyes rimmed in red. "I'm not going to hurt you so don't hurt yourself trying to get away from me." He was right, everything hurt, especially between my legs. I felt shame as tears began to gather in my eyes. "Can you tell me your name?"

I shook my head no. I could probably talk but I really didn't want to and I really didn't want anyone knowing my name. Silly maybe but it was mine and I was tired of people taking things from me.

"You don't have to tell me. I'm just gonna call you Pixie ok?" He was asking me permission? Just for that I would allow it. I nodded slightly, not taking my eyes from him. "Are you hungry?"

I watched him as I surveyed my body and all the aches and pains until I found the one I was looking for. The pain of hunger was distinct amidst the pain of bruises and cuts and trauma. I nodded again slightly and watched as he nodded back then stood and left the room, leaving the door ajar, not quite open but not quite closed.

"Knock knock," A feminine voice that was slightly familiar said from the hallway. "Hi dear, you probably don't remember me, I'm Edith. Aiden said you were awake, would you like help to the bathroom?"

My eyes flared as I thought about it and realized Edith was just in time. I nodded vigorously then winced at the pain and held my hand out to her.

"All right then dear, let's go." Edith said stepping into the room and taking my hand, helping me off the bed. "Don't want to talk yet, eh?" I shrugged and she left me in the bathroom.

Never in my life had going to the bathroom been painful but now it was. I carefully tidied myself and flushed then stepped to the door. When I opened it the guy was there with food, looking like he was way out of his element. Welcome to my life buddy.

Seether

Aw hell, was the only thought in my head when Pixie stepped

out of the bathroom. We had put her in my shirt last night because it seemed to be the only thing long enough to cover her but now seeing her standing up and wearing it was a bad thing.

Well, it was a good thing because I at least knew my cock still worked but it was a bad thing because I was getting turned on by this girl who had just been beaten and raped and looked like it.

"Your food," I said, handing her the plate and Edith the bottle of water and utensils. "Edith can help you if you need."

Then I turned tail and ran; that's right I'm a complete coward, I can admit it, this girl scared me. The guys didn't realize it but I had never had a girl in my room and it had been years since I'd had sex. It seemed that watching a woman get gang raped was a huge turn off for me, to the point that even four years later I still couldn't get it up. Fuck.

As I walked down the hall to the main room of the clubhouse I scratched the back of my head then at the last minute remembered to duck under the door jam. Shit sometimes I hated being 6'8".

It was near impossible to buy pants and shirts with long sleeves, my shoes were all custom made and cost a fortune and I could never find gloves big enough in the winter.

Sure, basketball was easy but that wasn't a career option for me. Teams generally don't like it when you completely freak out on the court in a PTSD episode and lose it on the fans.

I walked into Lo's office where I knew the other guys were waiting and slumped on the couch sighing deeply.

"How's the girl?" Lo asked quietly. All these guys had been outside last night when Little D had dumped her in front of our gates. I shook my head and sighed again. "She told you her name yet?"

"Nope, if she can talk she's refusing to. I asked her if it was ok if I called her Pixie and she agreed but I got the impression if I just started calling her that she wouldn't like it." I replied shrugging.

"Pixie?" Hammer asked, smirking.

I shrugged again, totally unconcerned with his teasing. "The red hair cut short like that and all spikey, she looks like a fairy or a pixie or something."

"She's had a lot taken from her and that's just what we know of in the last 10 hours." Axle said still shell shocked and thinking hard about what his mom, Edith, had revealed last night about her own nightmare. She got pregnant with Axle's sister, Hammer's fiancé from being raped and then out of desperation allowed a toxic person into their lives in the form of Axle's stepdad.

It had been a long year, with a member named Demon getting involved in a drug ring then dying after a bust gone wrong. We only found out months later that Demon left behind a daughter who was living with Lo's now fiancé Alana and her five kids. That had been an entertaining time watching them fall in love.

Then Kat, Axle's little sister had shown up out of the blue and knocked Hammer for a loop and they fell in love and were expecting triplets and Axle had fallen in love with Alana's friend Brooke and they were expecting a baby.

Of the four of us who were closest in the club I was the only one not attached to a woman. Mostly I was ok with that but I did wish I was able to have that kind of a relationship with a woman.

Hell, even without a woman. I'd tried homosexual sex but it just didn't work, nothing worked. At least I knew I wasn't gay, I didn't think anyway and it seemed that at least one woman could get me hard.

Too bad she was beaten so badly I could barely tell the colour of her skin and even her multitude of freckles were hidden. I hoped that wasn't what it took for me to get turned on, that would be a disaster.

"You think her throat was damaged like Hammer's?" Lo asked, nodding to the man. He had been in an IED attack during his last deployment into the SandBox and had just recently had his larynx repaired so he could talk normally again. "Or is not talking a choice?"

"Hard to say, Lo," I replied, shaking my head again. "It could be she isn't able to talk because of emotional or physical trauma, she does have at least a mild concussion, or it could be she just doesn't feel safe enough to talk to us yet. I just don't know."

"All right, we are not going to push her. I don't care if we wait ten years for her to tell us anything or if she leaves here one day without ever having said a word. I do however want her to know and understand that she is safe and she is free to leave once she heals as least physically. We need to show her that no matter what we are here for her if she needs us." Lo said looking at each of us, "However, having said that do you think she'd write anything down?"

"It's possible I suppose. I don't know if she's left or right handed but her left hand was broken up pretty bad. Edith didn't think anything was actually broken, just bruised and jammed bad enough that it would make using it difficult. I'll ask her when I go back; she was eating when I left."

"Maybe we should look at moving her to another room." Axle suggested clasping his hands behind his head.

"No, she stays in my room." I said adamantly, "She doesn't move until she asks to and no one asks her if she wants to." The three guys looked at me like I was nuts but they dropped it. "All that shit Demon left about CMNSS do you want me to look into it?"

"No, I don't think we need another shit storm on top of the one we already have." Lo answered, pinching the bridge of his nose. "Send it over to Sharpie and ask him to forward it to whomever he trusts to deal with it."

"I'll do it tomorrow."

"I think we're done here. I need some Alana family time." Lo said standing and stretching behind his desk. We all agreed it was still family time since it was Boxing Day and I still had to call my parents. Damn I loved my mom and dad and my brothers but I really was not looking forward to all the questions.

"Aiden do you have a girlfriend yet? How are you going to give me grandkids if you don't get a girlfriend? You'll never get a girl to marry you and give me grandbabies if you don't get out of your room and date Aiden. Look at your brothers, they both gave me grandbabies, when are you going to step up honey?"

Sorry mom, the plumbing didn't work.

I had tried many times to have sex once I got back. I tried with blond and redheaded girls with light coloured eyes thinking the more different they were from the girl in that hut the less likely I was to see her in my head.

That didn't work, though. Then I tried with a dark haired girl with dark eyes just like the girl in the hut, I almost threw up.

I tried Viagra, hello huge failure! I got it up all right but I couldn't go near the poor girl, and then the disaster at the gay club, what a mess.

Thankfully I had met a good friend there who completely understood how seriously fucked up I was and didn't hold it against me. We even still talk once in a while but at the moment he was going through his own shit and couldn't help me out right now. I sighed and went to find a quiet comfortable spot to call my parents, I was gonna be awhile.

CHAPTER 2

Grace-Lynn

I had been in this room for about a week now and Edith was the one bringing me my meals. That was fine with me, I wasn't ready to leave the confines of these four walls and she said it gave her a chance to check on me and my injuries.

I guess I was starting to look tired because Edith made me eat faster so she could leave. Then she left saying to get some rest. Hmm, perhaps I wasn't that great a conversationalist. That's ok, no one was going to make me do anything I didn't want to ever again, not even talk.

I looked over all of Aiden's computers with something akin to lust but not. I didn't think I would ever feel that again. Jealousy maybe was what I was feeling. He had a lot of impressive hardware.

I was about to get up and take a closer look when there was a knock on the door and he stepped inside. Damn he was tall. He would tower over even me, he was so tall and I was 5'11". Crazy, when I finally find a guy who was taller than me and I didn't want him.

"Uh, Edith said you were resting." He mumbled, shoving his big hands in his pockets.

I bet he had a hard time finding gloves in the winter. I just shrugged, even if I were talking, what would I say to that. He cleared his throat and looked everywhere but at me.

That was ok, if he wasn't looking at me then I could stare at him. He really was handsome, not the chiseled and hard kind of handsome of the other men I'd seen around here but handsome none-the-less.

"Are you left or right handed?" He suddenly asked. What the hell kind of question was that? My confusion must have shown on my face because he quickly explained. "We understand you may not want to speak and we're not going to make you. Can you speak?" I nodded and shrugged. "You're choosing not to?" I nodded again waiting for him to get mad and was shocked when he didn't.

"Ok," he said instead. "Do you know sign language?" I shook my head no. "Hmm, if I gave you a pen and paper would you write something for me?" I stared at him, wondering what he would ask me to write. "I won't ask your name, and anything I ask you can choose not to answer just like you are now." I shrugged and he handed me a pad of paper and a pen that was slightly chewed.

"Sorry about that," he said nodding to the pen, "Nervous habit. So, can you tell me how you ended up with Little Douche?" I raised my eyebrows at the name he had given Li'l D and the corners of my mouth quirked. "Yeah, we kinda don't like him; he's caused us a lot of problems." I nodded then wrote on the pad and held it up.

I know.

"You know," Aiden sighed then rubbed a hand down his face. "How do you know? What do you know?"

I'm D's hacker, I know everything.

"Well fuck, that kind of changes things." Aiden said, sighing. My eyes must have gotten big because he was quick to reassure me. "No, not for you, you're still safe. We will keep you safe no matter what. However this does mean that you could help us, too."

How?

"You know everything about him. You could help us bring down his organization and put this shit to an end." I must have looked apprehensive again because he kept talking. "Just giving us information, you would still be safe; you would just give us the intel we needed to take him down, you wouldn't even have to leave this room if you didn't want to."

"I like this room." I whispered blinking. "It's quiet and only you come in here."

"You have a beautiful voice." Aiden smiled sincerely. "You can stay in this room for as long as you want."

"But isn't this your bed?" I asked, confused.

"Yeah, but I don't sleep very well so I don't use it much. It's really all yours for at least another couple of days." He shrugged.

"You only sleep every couple of days?"

"Every four is my limit, then I sleep for eight hours, too exhausted to dream." He shrugged again like this was a totally normal way to live. Looking at him now I could see just how exhausted he was.

"Nightmares?" He shrugged yet again, like it was no big deal. I was baffled by this man. "How do you stay awake for four days?"

"Sheer will power and a lot of coffee." He smiled quietly. "So, you said you are a hacker, feel free to use any of my computers you want. It doesn't matter which one, they're all secure and I don't keep anything sensitive on these ones."

I smiled at him and nodded slightly but didn't leave the bed. He smiled again then got up and left the room, taking my dishes with him and I didn't see him for the rest of the day.

CHAPTER 3

Seether

"Seether man, what are you doing out here?" Lo asked, walking into the main room of the clubhouse. It had been a week since Pixie had spoken to me. "I don't think I've seen you out of your room this much in months."

Shit, I was hoping no one would notice. I didn't like being the center of attention, which is hard not to be when you're as tall as I am, and I knew someone was going to notice I was around more.

It wasn't that I was trying to avoid Pixie; I still didn't know her name even though she was talking to me now, it was more that I was stupid and I was avoiding Pixie. The other day when we had talked I had left my room and not gone back until she was already asleep.

Then I sat at my computers and tried to ignore that she was in my bed and her scent was all over my sheets.

Fuck, I was going to have to change my bed before I slept again or I would never get any sleep and then my four day cycle would be all messed up. Shit this was a disaster! Why the hell did I tell the guys to put her in my room?

There were empty rooms she could have stayed in but then I

couldn't keep an eye on her. It had been two weeks since she had been dumped in front of our gates and on my sleep days I had gone to one of the empty rooms to sleep.

This meant I really hadn't slept and had taken a sleeping pill which made me feel even worse than if I hadn't slept at all. I looked up again when Lo cleared his throat.

"What?" Shit, did he say something else and I didn't even hear it?

"Never mind, I need you to talk to your Pixie more about Li'l D, see if she can give you more info into his banking and supply runs and what not."

"Sure Lo, I'll do that now." I levered myself off the couch and walked across the room to the hall to the private rooms.

"Hey Seether, you ok?" Lo called to me and I could hear the concern thick in his voice.

"Yeah Prez, I'm good." I replied without turning.

"Getting close to that time of year hey?"

"Is it?" I asked, purposefully being obtuse.

"Get some sleep will ya? You look like shit."

"Will do Prez," I answered and left the room, leaving him behind staring I'm sure at my retreating back.

He was right, though. In six more days it would be the anniversary of that horrible day when I lay tucked up in a blind and watched a woman get gang raped. Nope, not going to sleep on that day and possibly not tonight like I had planned now that Lo had brought it to the forefront of my mind. Perfect.

***

"Hey Pixie," I said as I walked into my room a few minutes later. "I was wondering if you could – oh, no I'll come back."

"No, this is your room, you stay I'll go back into the bathroom." She said scrambling to hold her towel up and grab her clothes at the same time.

Stupid me, not thinking I was intruding on her I walked in as she was just dropping her towel from her shower to get dressed. Damn I'm an idiot. On a slightly happier note the bruises seemed to have faded a lot since she got here.

"I'm really sorry, I should have knocked."

"Don't be silly Aiden, this is your room." She said coming out of the bathroom, thankfully fully clothed this time, and drying her hair with a towel. "You shouldn't have to knock on your own door."

"Yeah, but my room is occupied by someone who needs and deserves privacy and I wasn't thinking that you might be naked in here."

"Oh, what were you thinking about?"

"Um . . . I was actually trying to get away from Lo."

"I thought Lo was your friend, why would you be trying to get away from him?"

"He is my friend, and technically my boss. He was just asking questions that I didn't want to answer and he brought up something I didn't want to talk about."

"Something you didn't want to talk about at all? Or something you didn't want to talk to him about?" I stared at her and realized she was right.

I didn't want to talk to Lo about it; I didn't want to talk to any of the guys about it. Deep down I felt like I should have been stronger or that I should have done something different, or as a sniper I should have been able to take out all five of those tangos.

"Good point. I don't want to talk to him about it."

"But you don't want to talk to me about it?"

"I don't know you."

"Maybe that's the point?" I thought about that for a minute. She was right; she didn't know me either so how could she judge me?

"It's gruesome and graphic and it will probably touch close to home for you."

"Because I was raped and these things that you can't let go is about rape? Were you raped?"

"No, not me I witnessed someone else being raped."

"Did you know this person?"

"No."

"Were you in a position to stop it?"

"Possibly."

"But . . .?"

"But I was ordered to hold both my position and my fire and I thought at the time I absolutely had to follow the orders of my superior officer."

"And you don't feel that way anymore?"

"I don't know." I said shrugging.

The whole conversation we had been staring at each other, never breaking eye contact. There was something in her clear gray eyes that was holding me hostage.

She wasn't asking for painful details just my feelings at the time and I was able to answer her honestly. Surprisingly my heart rate was no longer threatening to beat out of my chest anymore either.

"If you had not been ordered to stand down do you think you could have saved this person?"

"Maybe, it would have meant five precision kill shots. I was a pretty good sniper. Not the best mind you but still damn good."

"Five . . . kill shots?"

"Yeah, there were five tangos . . . they took turns." I stopped when I saw the colour drain from her already pale face making her freckles stand out more and I finally broke eye contact. "Sorry, too much information."

"No," She cried, reaching for me. "No it's ok. I asked and I guess compared to that poor woman?" she asked and I nodded, "compared to that poor woman I was lucky."

"Luck had nothing to do with it." I said shaking my head.

"Anyway, you haven't been sleeping here even on your fourth day and you don't look very good. I changed the sheets so you could have a clean bed and I'll go somewhere else." She said smiling.

"Oh, no it's ok. I mean yeah I would normally sleep tonight but now that Lo has brought that up and now we've talked about it I doubt I'll be able to sleep anyway."

"You should at least try, you look like you're about to fall over." I nodded and shrugged. "You're not going to, are you?"

I smirked, "Am I that easy to read?"

"Only because I've been sitting here for the last two weeks watching you." She replied shaking her head.

"Are you bored in here with just me all the time?" I asked, suddenly worried that I wasn't taking as good care of her as I thought I was. "There are other women here, besides Edith that is and they all want to meet you but I've been holding them off until you're more up for it, but then I guess I should have asked you if you wanted visitors."

"Stop!" she exclaimed holding her hands in front of her. "I have not been bored, at all. I have enjoyed the quiet and being able to hide in my head with just the hum of your computers to keep me company. I would like at some point to meet these other women but for now I am more than ok with just your company. That is if you're ok with that, I don't have to stay in here, I mean unless there's nowhere else for me to go." She stopped herself and took a couple of deep breaths, closed her eyes then opened them and looked at me with a touch more confidence.

"What I meant to say instead of babbling, is that I like being in your room and spending time with you however if you would like your space back and there is somewhere else I can go then I will gladly get out of your hair."

"No," I said shaking my head. "That won't work. I like you in my hair and in my space. I don't know why because since that day I just told you about, I haven't wanted to spend any time anywhere doing anything with a woman. You're ... comfortable and I like you being here."

"Ok, then I'll stay if that's what you want."

"I do, what do you want?"

"To stay."

Then stay."

"What about sleeping tonight?"

"I can go somewhere else."

"No Aiden, you can't, this is your room and your bed and you've been very sweet letting me use it but I won't interrupt your schedule anymore."

"It's ok, really." I said, but she was shaking her head adamantly. I sighed and looked up at the ceiling, hoping the answers I needed were up there . . . they weren't. "It is a king size bed, we could share it and not even breath each other's air. We could even build a wall between us if that would help you feel safe."

"I don't feel threatened by you Aiden. And yes, I would be fine sharing the bed. I am . . . apprehensive but I know you won't hurt me." I nodded and gestured towards the bathroom.

"I'm just going to have a shower then; I'll be out in a little while."

"Ok."

CHAPTER 4

Grace-Lynn

OK? I was not ok! What was I thinking? Sleeping with a man; all be it not having sex with him but still! I was raped not even a month ago! But I knew right away what the difference was. Yes I was raped, by a man, who never cared for me, by a man who was brutal and cruel and evil.

Aiden was none of those things. Aiden would never force himself on me, he didn't even force me to talk when I didn't want to and he didn't force me to tell him my name.

Instead he gave me a nickname, a ridiculous one given that I am as tall as I am, but I suppose to him I am pretty tiny.

I didn't realize I had been standing in the same spot staring at the bathroom door until the water shut off. I quickly hurried around to the other side of the bed and slid under the covers. What should I do? Pretend to be asleep, lay here staring at the ceiling?

Crap! Before I could decide the door opened, the light turned off and Aiden climbed into the other side of the bed, turned away from me and said goodnight.

Well hell! I guess I had nothing to be so freaking neurotic about! He wasn't going to make me have sex with him; I knew that; he just wanted to sleep for crying out loud! He only sleeps every four days, it's not like he's worried about me over here.

"Pixie?"

"Yeah?" I asked, nervous that I had done something to upset him.

"Shut your brain off, I can hear you thinking from here."

"Oh, sorry." I said, feeling sheepish. He sighed heavily then turned towards me.

"Don't be sorry, and don't be nervous. I'm not going to make you do anything. You can't do anything to upset me or make me angry. I'm not going to ask you to do anything either."

"Ok."

"Do you understand what I'm saying?"

"I think so?"

"No you don't, I suck at this shit and you're in no place to have me ask you this." He said, sounding exasperated. "Look, I would love to ask you to come over here or for us to meet in the middle and for you to let me hold you while we sleep. I would love to comfort you and just . . . cuddle. But I won't ask that. I won't turn it down but it will be because you want it, not the other way around. So, stop worrying that you're going to do some-thing I don't like or that I'll get mad or that I'll make you do something. I won't."

"Ok. For the record I knew you would never hurt me or force me to do something I didn't want to." I whispered, staring at him in the darkness. He just nodded and started to turn away from me. "I would like you to hold me, but I don't know if I'm ready for that. Could I maybe cuddle against your back? It's kind of cold over here."

He smirked at that but moved closer to the middle of the bed and turned his back to me. "Why do you call me Aiden?"

"It's your name isn't it?" I asked, confused as I snuggled into his heat.

"Yeah, but only Edith calls me that, even Alana's parents and Hammer's mom call me Seether."

"Seether?"

"Yeah my road name."

"Right cause you guys are a motorcycle club."

"I guess, I'm not sure why we keep calling ourselves that. Yes we ride motorcycles, but we aren't a typical MC. We don't do anything illegal and we're so far from a 1%ers club I don't know that we can be called an MC."

"Are you a club?"

"Yeah, I guess. We're more of a rehab for injured soldiers."

"Sure, that's your mission, but that's not what you are, that's what you do." I said touching his shoulder blade with a fingertip.

"Tickles," He said chuckling.

"Sorry,"

"No, don't stop, it's nice." He said and so I continued tracing his skin.

He didn't have any tattoos that I could see and he wasn't super heavily muscled like Lo and Hammer and Axle. I knew that to keep in shape he mostly jogged, only what he called jogging and what I called jogging were two totally different things.

I was naturally thin with a naturally high metabolism but even if it wasn't naturally high I still wouldn't exercise.

"So, why Seether? Do you like the band that much?" I asked,

going back to our original topic.

"No, I mean yeah I like them but no that's not why I picked the name, or rather why it was picked for me. I was really angry when I came home and the guys said I just constantly seethed." He shrugged slightly and sighed.

"Are you still that angry?"

"No, now I'm just . . . sad I guess, disappointed, frustrated. I don't even know anymore."

"Hmmm," I hummed brushing his hair from the nape of his neck. "Does it help at all to talk about it?"

"I never used to think so," He said, yawning. "But for some reason I'm not totally freaking out right now."

As he talked his words got slower and his breathing deeper, calmer. Eventually he was sound asleep and I stopped running my fingers through his hair. I snuggled into this back and sighed heavily but didn't fall asleep right away.

Honestly I had been sleeping for so long and I was finally starting to heal. I needed something to do now, tomorrow I would get out of this room and meet the other women Aiden had talked about.

I was ready for that, right?

Sure I was, I was sleeping with a man after being raped. I knew damn well this man would never hurt me in any way like the last one had but still. This should bother me shouldn't it?

Now I was even more confused. Why didn't touching Aiden bother me? I knew I wasn't really normal, but even I couldn't be over being raped in less than a month right? Like that's kind of unheard of.

Was I over being raped? Or was I just ok being with a guy I knew wouldn't or possibly couldn't force me?

Damn I messed up. Who could I talk to? I was a foster kid; I didn't have any family to go to except my little sister who I hadn't seen since we were babies.

And the system hadn't really been kind to me so I didn't even know who I would contact about this, who would I talk to? Damn, would Aiden know? Or maybe Edith?

Sleep, I must sleep. This could all wait until morning.

CHAPTER 5

Seether

Four weeks after that amazing night I woke up the next morning and Pixie was gone. She wasn't in the bathroom either and I was starting to get worried. I had woken up beside her more often than I thought I ever would, sleeping with her more of every fourth day than not. I quickly brushed my teeth and went to look for her.

I found her in the least likely place I could think of, Lo's office. She was sitting huddled in a corner of his couch watching Lo, Alana and Brooke talking. She looked up when I walked in the room and smiled but the other's ignored me so I went and sat with her.

"You ok?" I asked quietly, not wanting to distract the others. "You were gone when I woke up."

She nodded, "I'm fine. You were sleeping so soundly I didn't want to wake you. I decided today was the day I was going to get out." She smiled and looked over to the two women arguing with Lo.

"What are they fighting about?" I asked, tracing the freckles across her nose.

"Whether or not they should have a therapist come in to talk to me or if I should go out to see one." She replied shrugging.

"That's not what we are debating." Alana said rounding on us. "I am all for a counsellor or therapist coming in and spending time with you here Pixie, I just think a group session could be good too, but you have to leave the clubhouse for that."

"And while I agree that group counselling could be good I don't agree that it's safe enough for you to leave the clubhouse right now." Lo replied giving Alana a look that said stop arguing you know I'm right. They seemed to have a staring contest that I knew Alana would never win.

She finally sighed and her shoulders slumped. "Fine, no group sessions yet. So what are you doing about the threat against Pixie?" She demanded shoving her hands on her hips and glaring at Lo. He in turn smirked at her and snorted.

"I have passed all the information Pixie has given us on to the police and they are planning raids and arrests as we speak." Lo replied, his eyebrows lifting close to his hairline. "Unless you would like me out there searching for the Douche myself? I can't kill the little fucker but I can certainly make him hurt."

"No, I don't want you in trouble or in danger. If you say we're safe here and the kids are safe at school with prospects following us around then that's just going to have to be enough." She sighed dejectedly.

"Come here baby." Lo said, holding his hand out to her. She rounded the desk and fit herself on his lap against his chest. "I know you're worried, but we have this under control and everything will be back to happy in no time. The kids are safe, you are safe, Brooke and Kat and their babies are safe. Pixie is safe; we won't let anything happen to any of you."

"I know Lo but I still worry."

"I know baby." He kissed the side of her head then whispered something in her ear and she jumped up and left the room. He rubbed a hand over his face then stood and followed her. "See you guys later."

Brooke watched them go with a bemused look on her face then shrugged and followed them out with a little wave.

"Have you eaten yet?" I asked Pixie after the room had cleared out.

"No, I came out of your room and Alana directed me in here."

"You hungry? We've got a fully stocked kitchen."

"Hmmm, with bacon and eggs and toast?"

"For you? Absolutely." I grabbed her hand and pulled her off the couch and led her out to the kitchen.

I made her breakfast and coffee and made my usual concoction that drove Kat nuts but helped keep me awake for four days at a time and we sat quietly and ate. She sat and watched me the whole time I moved around the kitchen but didn't say a word. I looked up and found her staring at me still.

"What?"

"Grace-Lynn." She replied, her eyes squinting slightly.

"Your name?" I asked and she nodded slightly. "It's beautiful."

"I prefer Pixie, it's all yours." She said still watching me. "But I want to find my sister."

"Your sister? You have family?"

She sighed, "No not family. I was in foster care until three years ago but my younger sister was adopted instead of going into foster care. She would be almost seventeen now. But she's the reason I never changed my name and never let anyone shorten it. I hoped it was strange enough that if she was to look for me she would recognize it."

31

"Do you remember her name, her birthdate?" I asked sitting back in my chair.

"Her name is, or was Ash-Lynn, with a hyphen like mine, Ash-hyphen-Lynn, Grace-hyphen-Lynn. I don't remember her middle name but her birth date was August the year I started school. I remember being excited to tell my friends about my new baby sister. It was the following February that my mom od'd and I went into the system and she was adopted."

"I thought they tried to keep siblings together?"

"I don't know about that." Pixie said, shrugging. "I only know that I went to one family and she went to another and when I turned eighteen and tried to find her I was told she had been adopted and I couldn't see the records."

"I wonder if I could hack into the system."

"I tried but I'm sure you're a much better hacker than I am so maybe you would have more luck, I don't know."

"Don't let all the equipment in my room fool you, better equipped doesn't always mean just better." I said smiling. "I'll look into it and see what I can find and if that doesn't work then I'll ask Sharpie to look into it."

"Sharpie?"

"The club's lawyer, I don't think he normally does stuff like this but he's had to do all sorts of strange things in his career with the club."

"Let me guess, he's sharp as a tac?"

"Nah, well, I mean yeah but that's not where his name comes from. He just really likes Sharpie markers, never goes anywhere without at least one in his pocket." I chuckled as she snorted and shook her head. "Come on, you can help me start looking for your sister." I said holding my hand out to her.

"Would you mind if I used one of your computers for something while you look for Ash-Lynn?"

"Nope, I already told you they were yours to use as you wished."

She smiled up at me, "Thanks."

Grace-Lynn

I sat at Aiden's computer and looked at the screen. My fingers were on home row, ready to type whatever I wanted but nothing happened. I looked down at my hands and wondered what I was thinking, what did I want to search?

I looked back up at the monitor and the google search engine sat open and the cursor blinked at me from the search bar.

Finally I sighed and typed the very question I thought last night. 'Is it possible for me to be over being raped after four weeks?'

About 3,370,000 answers, that's great. There was a list of websites from where to report rape to Wikipedia to where to look for counselors. Why couldn't anyone just give me an answer? One website said life after rape could never be normal. I didn't really want normal, normal for me wasn't good.

I read article after article and all of them said in some way or another that I would never "get over" being raped, that life could get better but not ever be the same, that I would never be the same. One article said I could enjoy sex again but really each time was a crap shoot of whether or not I was going to enjoy myself or freak the fuck out. Fantastic.

"What are you searching?" Aiden asked from beside me. He didn't take his eyes off his own monitor but he asked all the same.

"Whether or not I'll ever be normal again." I replied, sighing.

"Hmm, you mean after being raped?"

"Yeah."

"Well, whether you are or not doesn't really matter. It's whether or not you can live with it and if you can make something of your future isn't it? Or is that too simplistic?"

"Have you learned to live with your trauma?" I asked, regretting my snarky tone immediately.

"No," He replied simply. "I don't know that I ever will, but my trauma is different than yours. I witnessed a rape yes, but you experienced it. Your body as well as your mind was violated."

"Thanks for reminding me."

"Sorry."

"No, I'm sorry. You didn't do it, you're trying to help and I'm being a bitch."

"You're allowed to be a bitch. You have that right." Aiden said looking over at me. He opened his mouth to say something else but there was a knock on the door. "Come in."

"Hey Seether, I need to speak to Pixie." Lo said sticking his head in the room. "The police want to talk to her about everything she told us."

"Oh," I said, shaking my head. "I don't think –"

"I'll be right there with you, I promise I won't leave you and if you need a break I'll make sure you get one." Aiden said taking one my hands and looking right in my eyes. "This will help catch Little D and getting him caught and put in prison is the best thing."

I looked at them both, moving my gaze from one to the other. They were both caring, kind men and I knew I would be ok if I was with them.

I nodded, "Ok."

I took the hand Aiden held out and he helped me to my feet. He held my hand all the way down the hallway and into Lo's office. We stepped inside and Lo went to sit behind his desk.

I didn't look at anyone as I walked in, noticing only that there were two other men already in the office. I walked over to the couch with my head bowed and sat then looked up at Aiden before looking around the room.

It was then I realized I knew one of the men. He was often at D's house giving him information about cases and busts and investigations. He was not a nice man and while he hadn't been at the house the night I was beaten he had often been at the house when D had new girls come in.

I was never involved in the girls or that side of D's business dealings but I knew what he was doing with them . . . and to them.

"No!" I screamed, jumping to my feet, suddenly broken out of my frozen state. Everyone else in the room jumped in shock at my outburst but only Aiden moved, stepping in front of me and blocking me from the other men.

CHAPTER 6

Seether

"What's wrong?" I demanded, stepping in front of Pixie and grasping her shoulders in my hands.

"He works for D." She whispered so quietly I almost didn't hear her. Her head was bowed and she was looking at my feet. I tucked my index finger under her chin and lifted her eyes to mine.

"Which one?"

"The blond." She said, tears welling in her eyes. Lo stepped to us then and eyed me.

She says he works for D. I signed, knowing it was unlikely the officers knew sign language.

"Fuck." He whispered then signed, *Act like we don't know; maybe we can catch him in something.*

I nodded then held Pixie tight and whispered in her ear not to be scared, that we would take care of her. She nodded then sat on the couch and stared at her hands clasped tightly in her lap.

"Well Mr. Winters, it would seem you have a person of interest in an investigation staying here at your clubhouse." The blond officer that Pixie had pointed out said.

For once in all the years I've known Lo he didn't correct the man on his name, he hated being called Mr. Winters.

"Is that so?" Lo asked without batting an eye. "From what I understand, if it weren't for this person of interest you wouldn't have any information on a certain criminal and if you got your heads out of your asses you'd have caught said criminal by now."

"That's hardly the case Mr. Winters." The officer said. "We need to take Ms. Cameron into custody."

"No." Lo and I said at the same time.

The officers wouldn't have seen the twitch of Lo's fingers when I interrupted, telling me to be quiet but I saw it. I shut my mouth and sat back on the couch, stretching my arm over Pixie's shoulders.

"I am afraid that those are the orders we have, Mr. Winters." The other officer said, glancing at Pixie and I and then back to Lo.

"Is Ms. Cameron under arrest?" Lo asked.

"Not at this time, no." The second officer said.

"Then she will be at the station in one hour with her lawyer to answer any questions you have. Or you can ask your questions here and now and leave." Lo said, his tone brooking no argument.

"Unfortunately that is unsatisfactory –"

"Fortunately I don't give a shit." Lo interjected. "Those are the options, take them or leave them, I don't care but Ms. Cameron will not be leaving here with anyone but the gentleman on the couch with her or her lawyer or myself. Those are the terms."

The blond officer opened his mouth to argue but his partner cut him off, "One hour Mr. Winters, not a second more."

Then he stood and nudged his partner to follow him out the

door. There was a bit of scuffle on the other side of the door, a sharp word and then the two men were gone.

"What the fuck is going on?" Lo demanded as he lifted his phone to his ear. "Yeah Sharpie, I need you to meet Seether and Pixie at the police station. They're demanding she go down to answer questions as a person of interest ... right ... an hour ... ok, he'll be there with her, thanks. He'll meet you there." Lo said, hanging up the phone. "Go now; be early if you can but relax Pixie, Sharpie isn't going to let anything happen to you."

Pixie nodded then looked at me for reassurance. I tried to smile and give it to her but I don't think I succeeded. I took Pixie's hand and led her back to my room.

I grabbed my wallet and the keys to my bike, and then I looked at her and realized I hadn't thought about what this would mean for her. She hadn't been out of my room for almost four weeks and then only for a couple of days and now we were asking her to go out in public.

"Are you ok with this?" I asked, somewhat belatedly.

"With being a suspect or with talking to the police?"

"Well, both I suppose but I meant more leaving the clubhouse all together."

"Then no, I am not ok with this but I don't really have a choice. You will be with me all the time right?" She asked looking up at me with so much hope.

"I will try to be with you at all times. If I'm not Sharpie will be and he will keep you safe. He won't let anything happen to you, I promise." I touched her cheek with a fingertip then brushed a strand of hair off her forehead. "Do you want to take my bike or my truck?"

"I can ride on your motorcycle?"

"Yeah, it might not be super comfortable because I had it custom made for my height but we can give it a shot and we need to dress in a few extra layers since its January. Luckily we haven't gotten any snow yet this year."

"Yes please, I would very much like to ride on your motorcycle." She smiled so sweetly at me I felt like I had won the lottery, and there it was again, my cock rising to attention.

What the hell was it about this girl that had my dick looking for action? She wasn't bruised and battered anymore and my dick still liked her. She still acted like a victim when we were around other people, even the women but that was to be expected right?

When we were in Lo's office and she sat on the couch she made sure she was curled in the far corner away from everyone else. The same for the couch in the main room and she didn't stay out there if more than four or five people were there.

We walked out to my bike and I fitted an extra helmet on her head, tightening the straps and adjusting the latches then climbed on my bike and helped her on the back. She snuggled her thighs up tight against my hips and we were off.

"Are you comfortable?" I asked through the mike in my helmet.

"Oh, I can hear you!"

"Yeah the helmets are connected by Bluetooth so we can all talk whenever we're riding together, makes it a little safer."

"Wow, um yes I'm comfortable, this is great. Thank you for suggesting this."

"My pleasure, I would much rather ride my bike then drive my truck but I wanted you to be comfortable. I know Alana and Brooke haven't been on Lo and Axle's bikes and it's been awhile since Kat was on Hammer's, but that has more to do with her being pregnant." I replied, shrugging a bit and slowing for a red light.

After that we rode in silence, each just enjoying the air in our faces and freedom being on a bike gave us. The trip to the station wasn't long and we arrived well within the hour limit we were given.

"I'm glad you're here early." Sharpie said walking up once I'd parked and shut off the bike. Pixie and I took our helmets off and I helped her off the bike.

"Sharpie, this is Grace-Lynn Cameron, call her Pixie." I said introducing them to each other.

"It's nice to meet you sweetheart." Sharpie said, holding his hand out to her. She looked at it then shook it and smiled but didn't say anything. "So I've talked to one of the cops that was at the clubhouse today, the darker haired one. He said he didn't know why his partner had such a hard on for Pixie, his words, and it made no sense since she had A) given them invaluable information, and B) wasn't mentioned in any report about D incriminating or otherwise."

"Then why are we here?" I asked irritably.

"I don't know but I dragged the partner into the chief's office and had it out with them both. The partner, Constable Harmon, mentioned that he had long suspected his partner of being at least a little dirty and he thought this might prove it. The chief agreed to let it play out but only until Pixie had enough."

"Well then let's go home 'cause I've had enough and I haven't even gone inside." She said turning to me.

"Sorry Pix, we gotta go in there and get this finished. Little D has hurt a lot of people besides you and this has to stop." I said giving her shoulder a squeeze.

"I know." She sighed, resigned. "Let's get this over with then."

We went inside, following Sharpie and were put in an interrogation room. There was a huge one-way mirror on one wall but I mostly ignored it. We were left sitting in that room for close to forty-five minutes before the blond cop came into the room.

I was about to tell Sharpie the guy had five before we were walking out. As soon as he came through the door Pixie tensed and folded into a ball in her chair.

CHAPTER 7

Grace-Lynn

"Sorry that took so long, was reading a particularly good article in the bathroom." The cop said as he sat across the table from us. "Well Ms. Cameron, I see you brought your biker boyfriend and his disreputable lawyer with you."

"Your comments are unnecessary and inappropriate." Sharpie said, showing no reaction to the cop's words.

"Right." He said, drawing the word out. "My name is Constable Michaels, Ms. Cameron, you are here because you are under suspicion for your work with Little D, a notorious drug dealer."

"I'm pretty sure Little D is too small-time to be considered notorious." Sharpie deadpanned. "And just what exactly is my client suspected of?"

"Well, it would seem that Ms. Cameron was involved in quite a lot of illegal computer hacking, is that true Ms. Cameron?"

"No." I said quietly.

"No? That's it, no explanation?"

"There's nothing to explain. You asked if I was involved in illegal computer hacking, the answer is no."

"Ok, and how about the video surveillance of your boyfriend's clubhouse are you telling me you didn't hack into that?"

"Yes, I am telling you that. I built a camera that one of Little D's men mounted outside the clubhouse that would see inside through one of the windows."

"Did you know what that camera would be used for?"

"Not at the time no, D said he was going to use it to monitor security in his house. I built it, gave it to him and never saw it again."

"Really, you expect me to believe that?"

"I don't expect you to believe or not believe anything Constable. That's the truth."

"Uh huh, how about the girls?" the cop asked, shuffling some papers.

"D often had prostitutes in the house; I had nothing to do with them. I wasn't allowed to talk to him and if they tried to talk to me they wouldn't get paid so they stayed away from me."

"What about the report that says you dealt with their buyers?"

I paused for a moment, shocked by his question. "If there actually is a report that says that then it's false. I never bought or sold any person, I designed a book keeping program that D could use easily and kept track of the security cameras. That was all."

"I highly doubt that was all, you were Little D's girlfriend were you not? You sure like to hop beds."

Aiden moved like he was getting ready to reach across the table and kill the Constable but I put a hand on his arm to stop him.

"First of all I was not D's girlfriend. He tried many times to get me to go to bed with him but that was never something I wanted. Then he raped me four weeks ago and dumped me in front of the gates of the War Angels MC clubhouse. Aiden is not my boyfriend but my friend and has been taking care of me since my assault." I explained more for Aiden's benefit than this stupid cop.

"Right, are you reporting the alleged assault?" The Constable asked, making a note in his file.

"No, I am not reporting the actual assault. Now I am done answering your questions, I'm leaving."

"No Ms. Cameron you are not." The Constable said standing.

Sharpie and I both stood as well, both of us angry but Sharpie hiding it better than I was.

"Is my client under arrest?" Sharpie demanded.

"Not at this time but –"

"But nothing, if you are not arresting her then we are leaving." Sharpie said dismissively and led us out of the room and out of the station.

We kept going until we stood next to my bike and none of us spoke until I started helping Pixie with her helmet again.

"I'm sorry about that Grace-Lynn –"

"Pixie." I corrected Sharpie.

"Pixie, you handled yourself very well. You should be proud of yourself." I smiled slightly and shrugged.

I didn't feel proud. I felt dirty and embarrassed.

"I'm going to go back in to talk to the chief and see what can be done about Constable Michaels. Put him out of your mind. I'm going to have Sherri call you and get you both over for dinner one night. Don't worry, we'll order in, Sherri can't cook."

"Who's Sherri?" I asked Aiden as Sharpie walked away and back into the station.

"His wife, he's right, she's a horrible cook but don't tell her I said that." Aiden said smiling. "Come on let's go for a ride before we go back to the clubhouse. You're not too cold are you?"

I shook my head no; it was really only 4°C so not really cold but for sure far colder than it was in the summer around here. I found though, that if I was snuggled up to Aiden I didn't feel the cold air as it rushed past us.

We climbed on the bike and were quickly on our way out of the city. We didn't go far but in the opposite direction of the club-house which was west towards Monte Lake.

Instead Aiden took us north towards Barriere but stopped long before we got here and pulled off the highway just past Rayleigh at Vinsulla. We drove a little bit until we got to the edge of the Thompson River and just sat.

"This is pretty." I said looking around. "Why here?"

"I had no destination in mind. I didn't want to go all the way to Barriere but I wanted a quiet spot by the river."

"What are your plans for me out here Mr. Morgan?"

"Hmmm," He hummed with a smile. "No plan, just wanted to be with you. No pressure, just hanging out. You don't even have to talk, hell you don't have to sit here with me if you want to go for a walk or you want to sit quietly. Or if you'd rather we can get back on the bike and leave."

"You'd really do that? After driving all the way out here you would climb back on your bike and drive home just because I said so?"

"Absolutely." He replied with conviction.

"Why would you do that?" I asked on a whisper.

"Because I care about you and I want you to be happy." He answered just as quietly.

"Do you want to kiss me?"

"Yes but I won't."

"Not even if I ask you to?"

"Maybe but I doubt it. I want to make sure you're ready. I don't want to rush you."

"What if I want to rush you?"

"Rush me into what?"

"When was the last time you had sex, Aiden?"

"It's been awhile."

"Since before what you saw right?" Instead of answering he just nodded. "And how long ago was that?"

"Five years next week." He answered, dipping his gaze away from me.

"Look at me please?" I begged, so quiet I wasn't sure he heard me but he lifted his gaze to mine. "You have nothing to be ashamed of."

He shrugged and looked away again and then sighed. Reaching out I took his hand in mine and just held it, looking out over the water.

"I want a relationship with you Aiden. I just don't know what I'm capable of."

"Like I said, I care about you and for the first time in yes, five years, I am actually thinking about sex with a woman, you. But I won't pressure you into anything. Not kissing, not petting not sex not anything. When you're ready for whatever you're ready for we'll try it. But not before you say so."

"I read in an article earlier today that sex may not ever be normal. It could be years down the road and many successful tries in a row and I could just suddenly freak out. Are you ready for that?"

"No, are you?"

"Hell no," I snorted.

"Then we'll figure it out together. If we are starting something or doing something and you suddenly feel uncomfortable just say so and I'll stop. If you're too scared to say it and you freak out I know it's not about me and I'll be ok with that."

I smiled and suddenly shivered.

"Come on, let's get you back to the clubhouse and warm."

CHAPTER 8

Seether

"Seether!" Axle called as I walked into the kitchen. "What you been up to, man?"

It had been a month since Pixie and I had been into the police station to talk to Constable Michaels. Axle had been in and out of the clubhouse the last few weeks with his fiancé Brooke. Most often they stayed here at the clubhouse because he wanted to make sure she was safe but she really wanted to be at her house.

Brooke was three weeks away from giving birth to their first child and miserable. Although not nearly as miserable as Kat was pregnant with triplets and two months left to go.

"Not much man." I replied sipping my coffee. I was only putting eight teaspoons of sugar in it these days instead of ten and it still tasted bitter to me. "Just hanging out while Pixie visits with the women."

"Yeah I heard. I just dropped Brooke on the couch in the main room. God I can't wait for this pregnancy to be over!"

"Brooke driving you nuts?" I snorted, smirking at him.

"Nah, that's the easy part, just gotta give her anything she wants. No, I can feel Imogen kicking now and I just want to hold her and see her. And I sound like a fucking pussy." Axle exclaimed, pulling at his hair.

"Nah," I said chuckling. "You sound like a guy in love with his kid and his woman."

"When are you gonna get a woman? Or is that Pixie?"

I shrugged, not really sure how to answer. "I care about Pixie, but she's had it rough. It's only been two months."

"True, but she sleeps in your bed every night, and you sleep with her when you have your fourth night nap." I looked at him somewhat shocked. "You think we didn't know you only slept every four nights? You must also think we're dumb enough not to know why you drink your coffee the way you do. You actually think we don't know why your sleeping habits are what they are? We know brother, and we got your back. The nightmares suck . . ."

"I can't take pills. I hate the way they make me feel. I'd just rather not sleep but unless I'm falling down exhausted then I dream and I can't live through that again."

"I get it man; I've had more than my fair share. We see some horrible shit over there. What about Pixie, she having nightmares?"

"Not recently." I replied, shaking my head. I hadn't really thought about it actually. She did still sleep in my bed and I loved it.

The few times I did sleep she had to be there and I had to ask her not to change the sheets first because I couldn't sleep unless I was surrounded by her scent. She thought I was nuts and I probably was.

Pixie still cuddled into my back when I slept in the bed but more often than not by morning I was turned facing her and holding her in my arms.

49

"Uh, excuse me guys." Pixie said from the doorway. "I'm sorry, I don't mean to interrupt, I just . . . need to . . ." she didn't finish what she was saying just walked quickly towards me across the room.

I was sitting at the table and she bent at the waist, laid her hand on my cheek and kissed me sweetly on the lips. Then she turned and ran out of the room and I sat and stared after her, letting a slow smile stretch my lips as Axle howled with laughter.

Grace-Lynn

I don't know how I get myself into these things. One minute I'm sitting on the couch in the main room with Alana, Brooke and Kat and the next thing I know I'm running for the kitchen like my pants are on fire.

It wasn't my fault, really. Alana and Kat dared me to do it. Thinking back on it I should have known it was coming. It all started with Alana's strange question . . .

"What's your favourite thing about being pregnant?" She asked looking specifically at Brooke and Kat.

"The sex." They both said together. I snorted and I'm pretty sure the sip of Diet Coke I'd just taken flew out my nose.

"What?" Kat demanded, "Seriously, I mean there are other things like the babies kicking or knowing there's life growing inside me –"

"A lot of life." Brooke interjected smirking and rubbing her own bulging belly.

"Shh you. But really, everything is so much more sensitive and it's really, really great."

"I agree, with the first one anyway. After that you're so tired you're lucky if you have sex anymore." Alana said, shrugging and smiling. "What about you Pixie?"

"I wouldn't know, I've never been pregnant." I replied shrugging.

"Ok then, what was your favourite thing about being with a guy?" Alana amended. I thought for a minute but didn't really need to.

"Kissing." I said decisively.

The other three women hummed appreciatively, each thinking of their own men.

"Who are you kissing?" Kat asked, raising an eyebrow.

"No one."

"That's a shame." Alana muttered under her breath.

"Pixie is there someone you would like to be kissing?" Brooke asked gently.

I didn't say anything but apparently the look on my face was enough of an answer.

"It's Seether isn't it?" Kat demanded smiling and laughing.

I smiled shyly and shrugged. What was I going to say? No? These women could read a lie a mile away.

"You should go do it right now," Alana said sitting forward. "He's in the kitchen, just go lay one on him."

"Oh no, I couldn't." I said shaking my head sure that my fear was plain on my face.

"Oh yes you could and you should." Alana replied.

"What does your therapist say about this stuff?" Brooke asked, curbing Alana's enthusiasm for a moment.

"That I'll know when I'm ready to do stuff and try stuff and not to feel like I'm wrong or bad because I want to. She said masturbation was a good way to see if I was even interested in sex."

I said meekly, knowing my face was bright red. I was a redhead after all, I blushed easily.

"Whooeee!" Kat cried laughing. "Have you done it?"

"What? Masturbate?"

"Kat, that's a bit private." Brooke said coming to my rescue.

Kat just shrugged and looked at me so I shrugged back and nodded. It's not like it was a big deal. Aiden had a massaging showerhead in his bathroom, and I'd heard it can be … stimulating so I tried it. The reports were not wrong.

"All right," Alana jumped in, "I dare you to go into the kitchen and kiss Seether on the lips. Just a peck, I'm not talking about tongues and all that, just a kiss."

And that's how Aiden and I ended up having our first kiss. I was dared to do it and right after I did it I ran right to our room and hid. I wasn't scared, I was embarrassed.

I was twenty-one years old and I felt like a thirteen year old with my first crush. Maybe that's how I had to look at this. Maybe this had to be a completely new experience with none of the stuff from the past.

It didn't take long after I was hidden away that Aiden knocked on the door and stepped inside. He didn't come towards me, though. He stood at the door and watched me, waiting for me to make a move, any move.

"I'm sorry." I blurted.

"Why?" He asked, confused.

"I embarrassed you."

"No," He replied, shaking his head. "You made me happy, but not embarrassed."

"Oh." Now I was confused. "Did you like it?"

"Yes."

"Do you want to do it again?"

"Yes, very much."

"Right now?"

"Only if you want to." Aiden responded nervously, fisting and re-laxing his hands.

"I do . . . want to kiss you again." I said wringing my hands.

He stepped towards me then stopped and looked at me care-fully. My eyes stayed on his and he continued towards me then his big hand was tucking around the back of my head and his lips were on mine and it was the most amazing feeling I'd ever felt.

Aiden had the softest lips yet they were firm and in control. I could taste his coffee even though he kept his mouth closed over mine and I wanted to taste more of him so I slipped my tongue between my lips to touch his and he gasped and pulled back, his eyes slightly glazed and boring into mine.

Then there was no space between us and his lips were on mine again and his mouth was licking into my mouth and he tasted so sweet. My hands fisted in his shirt and I whimpered into his mouth as he wrapped an arm around my waist.

Slowly he pulled back and left gentle but scorching kisses on my lips and then my cheeks and nose and finally my forehead. Then he pulled me tighter to him and rested his chin on top of my head and breathed deeply trying to calm his racing heart.

"I knew you'd be sweet." He whispered as he rubbed my back. I was suddenly elated.

CHAPTER 9

Seether

For some reason I was exhausted. It had only been two days since I slept last and I shouldn't be this tired yet. I was sitting at my computers with my back to Pixie who was sleeping soundly. It was about ten at night and I was having trouble keeping my eyes open.

I almost wondered if someone had slipped something into my coffee when I remembered I wasn't drinking as much as usual and it didn't have as much sugar as it usually did. I looked at my mini fridge and thought about getting out a red bull then looked over at Pixie sleeping peacefully in my bed.

I couldn't resist, I pulled off my shirt and slipped out of my pants and climbed in beside her.

She didn't wake up except to snuggle into me and sigh. I turned towards her and kissed her forehead then closed my eyes and within seconds I was sound asleep.

I don't know how long I slept, I remember Pixie getting restless in her sleep and I shushed her and threw a leg over hers. She seemed to settle almost immediately, or so I thought and I fell back asleep, only to be awoken sometime later by screaming.

My eyes immediately sprang open and I jumped off the bed,

looking everywhere for whatever it was that was making Pixie scream. As soon as I left the bed, though she stopped and there was no one else in the room. I turned to her and took in her frightened, tear stained face and her heavy breathing.

"What happened?" I demanded. "Did you have a nightmare?" I was panting, too and as I watched her she nodded. I moved to sit on the bed and she whimpered and tried to move away from me. "What did I do?"

She shook her head and swallowed deeply, gasping for breath. She sniffed and wiped the tears off her cheeks then hiccupped once more before closing her eyes and trying to calm herself. Fuck I felt like such a dick for scaring her.

"You didn't do anything." She whispered as she opened her eyes. "I think I was having a nightmare and I didn't expect you to be in the bed. And then you had your leg over mine and I couldn't move."

"Oh God," I said, rubbing my hands over my face. "God Pixie, I'm so sorry. I didn't even think. You were restless so I did throw my leg over yours to calm you, I didn't even think you would be scared by that. I'm so sorry."

"It's not your fault, Aiden. It's D's fault." She said on a sob.

"I know, but that doesn't mean I don't have to be careful not to scare you. And you didn't know I was coming to bed so you weren't expecting me to be there, I'm sorry I scared you baby." She nodded and wiped her eyes again. "What can I do? How can I fix this?"

She shook her head this time but smiled just a little. "You can't fix it, I'm broken and I won't ever be normal again."

"I don't want you normal. I lo – like you just the way you are. You're perfect how you are. I can't imagine any other girl being ok with my weirdness." She snorted but smiled just a little bit

55

more. "Can I hold you?"

Her eyes flared wide and she shook her head no. "Can I lie against your back though?"

"Of course, I'm getting in now ok?" She nodded and waited for me to get comfortable and I could feel her holding her breath then she snuggled in close and I could feel her warm wet breath on the back of my neck.

I never thought I would find that comforting.

Grace-Lynn

Did Aiden almost say he loved me? Did I imagine that or was that for real? Was I stupid to think that was possible? I really wanted to believe that was possible but I was afraid I had heard it because I was broken and no one had ever said it to me.

I mean, I'm sure my mom did when I was little but she died when I was five and I don't remember her almost at all. What I do remember was not a loving joyful woman.

I sighed heavily and finally let myself drop off to sleep, snuggling deep under the covers and against Aiden's back. He smelled so good, and I knew in my heart and logically that he was safe even though my nightmare told me otherwise.

It was late morning when I finally woke up again and I was alone in the bedroom. I didn't know where Aiden was and that was probably a good thing. I was embarrassed enough as it was. I quickly jumped up and rushed into the bathroom to get ready for the day.

I had an appointment with my therapist today and was sort of looking forward to it. I had been seeing this therapist once a week for the last month and a half and I really felt like I was making progress. Or at least I thought I was until that nightmare last night, but the kiss before that was progress right? Especially since I initiated it?

I just didn't know anymore. I had a new normal and I was still trying to figure out what that was. So, while I was in the shower I did make myself orgasm. Another step toward normal . . . I think, or rather towards my new normal.

Yes I might continue to freak out and I might continue to have nightmares but I was going to make sure my body and my mind recognized that a man's touch was enjoyable, pleasurable, not painful and hurtful. I had a plan, but I wanted to find out what my therapist thought of it first.

I'm sure now that Aiden was actually going to say he loved me or that he loved something about me but changed his mind at the last second. I knew I was worthy of his love, but I wanted to know that his love for me wasn't from pity.

I was sitting in an empty room with my therapist an hour later as she asked me questions and I answered them as honestly as I could. Really there were things I just couldn't tell even her. I couldn't tell her how I felt when D raped me; I could tell her the physical feelings, the pain but not the emotions. I couldn't explain that either.

"Do you want to hear my plan?" I asked suddenly.

"Of course." Margaret said smiling.

"I've decided I'm going to make a new normal for myself. I'm going to reconstruct my life from what I have right now and I'm going to build it up from right now." I said proud of myself.

"I think that's a great idea but I think you should still be taking it slowly." She replied pensively.

"I know, I'm not rushing into anything I promise. I just feel like for the first time in my life I have a future. When I was with D I was just there, existing day to day but now I feel like I have something to look forward to."

"That's great Grace-Lynn. Does any of this plan have to do with Aiden?"

"Yeah, most of it. I think he almost told me he loved me last night but then changed his mind at the last minute. It was weird but really I'm not surprised. He's known me two months and most of that time I was scared and bruised and hiding in a corner. Now I'm just scared and hiding in a room but not the corner. I want him to love me and I want to love him but I want him to love me because he loves me, not because he pities me or feels bad for me."

"Hmm," Margaret hummed and nodded then jotted a note in her book.

"What does that mean?"

"It doesn't mean anything. I do think you've made a good plan for your future as long as you're doing it for you and not for Aiden. You should get better or healthy or strong or whatever for yourself, not for another person."

"I know, and I agree and I'm going to try really hard to do this for me because it's what I need but I do want to be with Aiden. I don't want to be with him to get that stuff over with, I want to be with him because it's him."

"That makes sense. I think you're being smart about this. We are out of time though and I have another appointment at my office I need to get to. I want you to try out a few of the things you have planned. Think small though, less is more. It's exciting that you kissed and that you're finding the pleasure that can be in sex again especially without a man involved. Keep that up. If you're sure that Aiden won't push for anything past kissing and he's open to it then keep it up. You need to do what feels good and you need to know the difference for yourself what is good and what is bad."

"Thanks Margaret." I said and hugged her then walked her out to the front door. When I turned around Aiden was standing beside the bar smiling at me. "What's that look for?"

"I found something about your sister." He stated, then waited for me to react.

"What? Show me! You have to show me!" I cried running to him and grabbing his hand, trying to drag him back to our room.

"Ok, ok relax. I don't know what it is yet, if anything but I possibly found her school."

"Really? So you have a picture of her?"

"Maybe, if it is her." We walked into our room and sat in our chairs at his computer desk. "First of all, did you know that Cameron is your mother's maiden name?"

"Yeah, that's why I could never find my dad. I didn't know who he was. His name wasn't on my birth certificate and I couldn't get Ash-Lynn's. He left right after my mom found out she was pregnant and refused to have an abortion."

"Well, believe it or not, I found an Ashlyn Cameron at the same school that Alana's kids go to. It's a small school so Nate probably knows her."

"What? How can her last name be Cameron?"

"Did you know your mom's brother, your uncle James Cameron?"

"No, mom always said she didn't have any family."

"Well it looks like your uncle and his wife adopted your sister, and possibly couldn't have kids of their own because there weren't any to follow your sister. Mind you I have no proof of this, it could be all nothing but that's what I've found so far."

"This is crazy!" I exclaimed, pushing out of my chair and pacing.

"Why would they adopt Ash-Lynn and not me? I was only five, I wasn't that old!"

"I don't know, but if you want I can find out for you. I have all your aunt and uncle's information and I will be more than happy to go and ask him."

I looked at Aiden at first devastated that I wasn't good enough to be adopted by my uncle and then angry that he didn't take me, too.

"I want to go with you." I demanded shoving my hands on my hips.

"Um, I think it might be better if I meet him and see if he really is your uncle and if he's not then no harm no foul right?"

"Yeah, right I guess." Although I didn't really see why I had to be understanding of a man who had potentially tossed me to the wolves but fine, I would do it Aiden's way for Aiden.

CHAPTER 10

Seether

I stood outside the large home in Batchelor Heights, a rather expensive area of our city. It was a newer subdivision in the Batchelor Heights area that boasted larger houses and yards that were probably all taken care of by landscaping companies. I rang the doorbell and waited.

James Cameron, whether he was Pixie's uncle or not, was a dentist and could easily afford this house and the landscapers. His wife didn't work but was on many charitable foundations.

I was about to ring the doorbell again when the door opened and I was greeted by a tiny woman with platinum blonde hair and her roots needed to be touched up. At first she stared at my chest just below my breast bone then very slowly, like the Friendly Giant she looked way up. When her gaze finally rested on my face she gasped slightly and took a step back.

"I apologize for frightening you ma'am." I said politely. "My name is Aiden Morgan, I have urgent business with your husband. Is he available?"

"Oh," She exclaimed and turned to look behind her. "I suppose he is. Please come in out of the cold and I will see if he's free."

She smiled at me and I thought this woman must be stupid letting a strange man of my size into her home with no more information than my name. Then I looked around a little more and I saw the armed guard standing beside the door. I nodded to him but made no effort to speak to him and turned to face forward while I waited.

"Aiden Morgan?" I heard from the back of the house. "I don't know an Aiden Morgan."

"Well dear, this gentleman seems to know you and he says his business is urgent." The wife said, obviously trying to placate the man.

"Who the hell has urgent business with a dentist?" I couldn't agree more, usually. "Who the hell are you really?" The older man demanded coming to a stop in front of me. He wasn't really old, maybe in his mid-fifties and he seemed to be in good shape, his hair was trim and he was dressed well.

"I really am Aiden Morgan sir. I am a friend of your niece's." I said calmly.

Mr. Cameron sighed and hung his head. "I figured someone would be coming sooner or later. Come on back to my office young man." I followed Mr. Cameron to his office and waited until he closed the door before addressing him.

"So, you are the uncle of Grace-Lynn Cameron and you adopted her younger sister Ash-Lynn?"

"Yes. How did you find out about the girls?" He asked motioning for me to sit on the leather couch while he took a seat in one of the matching arm chairs.

"Before we get into that, I need to know why you adopted one girl and not the other." I said getting right to the heart of my visit. The old man sighed heavily again and rubbed his eyebrows with his finger and thumb.

"Seventeen years ago I was married to my first wife. When she heard that my sister Evelyn had died and her girls needed homes she agreed to take the baby but not the older girl. I regretted letting her make that decision ever since. I've tried to find Gracie since then but I never could."

"Grace-Lynn, she hates being called Gracie." I said automatically.

"Sorry, how did you meet Grace-Lynn?"

"I met her when her battered and beaten body was dropped outside the front gates of the compound of the War Angel's MC Christmas night." I said plainly, I didn't believe in beating around the bush and I had yet to decide if this man deserved my sympathy. When he gasped and dropped his head into his hands I thought maybe I was a bit too harsh.

"She was beaten?"

"Yes, and raped. After she had been let go from foster care at eighteen she had nowhere to go so she got involved in a gang. She didn't get into drugs or anything like that but she's smart and she can hack a computer faster than anyone I know, even me and I'm damn fast. The dealer she was involved with decided he didn't need her anymore and he was looking for ways to hurt our club. Apparently this was a good way to do that." I shrugged.

"And how is she now? It's almost the end of February, is she doing ok now?"

"For the most part, she's still traumatized and has nightmares some nights but she's getting through it. She sees a counsellor every week, in fact she just had a session yesterday and she's been in good spirits." I explained, knowing I wasn't even scratching the surface. "She's been looking for Ash-Lynn since she turned eighteen but was told because her sister was adopted the files were closed."

"I talked to my current wife about trying to find Grace-Lynn again and she was all for it. She, my wife, was in a car accident a few years ago after we got married and she's not really recovered all her mental faculties since. You may have noticed how easy it was to get into the house?" I nodded, "I'm not super important but I worry for my wife and daughter and their safety, hence the security guard . . . can we meet Grace-Lynn?"

"She would like that very much. Well, she wants to see her sister but she has questions. She's confused and angry." I said standing. "I would like to bring her back tomorrow but I know she won't wait that long so if you're ok with it I'll be back in about an hour with her. I had to bribe her to stay at the clubhouse."

"Of course Mr. Morgan, please bring her over as soon as possible. I've always been honest with Ashlyn, we do spell her name differently now but we kept it the same. She knows she has an older sister and we were trying to find her. She will be happy to meet her."

I nodded and left the office then hurried out to my truck. I called Pixie on the way out to the clubhouse and told her to get ready because I was about to pick her up and take her to meet her sister.

Grace-Lynn

I couldn't believe it! Aiden had actually found my sister! I wondered so many times what she looked like now, what colour her hair and eyes were and now I was about to find out. I had changed about six different times by the time Aiden got to the clubhouse. When he walked into his room all the clothes he had bought me were all over the bed.

"For fuck sakes Pixie, it's your sister, do you really think she cares what you look like?"

"I don't know! I haven't seen her since she was an infant!" I screamed back at him completely frustrated. "I don't know anything about her!"

I could feel tears welling in my eyes and he took pity on me and turned to the closet. He pulled out a new pair of skinny jeans that I hadn't worn yet because I had nowhere to wear them to and a soft lavender coloured fitted sweater.

"Put these on," He said handing me the clothes, "Spike your hair a little, I like it like that and meet me out front in five minutes, you only need lip gloss, no makeup." Then he turned as was gone. I stood and stared at the door for a minute and jumped when he knocked on the door and called through it. "Four minutes, hurry the fuck up!"

I quickly got dressed and grabbed a pair of heeled short boots from the closet and pulled them on as I rushed to the truck. The whole way I nervously played with the radio, flipping from one station to the next finally stopping on a country station that was playing a song I liked.

"Oh no! No fucking way!" Aiden said reaching for the radio.

"Hey, I like that song!" I said trying to swat his hands away.

"I don't care. There is to be no country music in my truck."

"But I like country."

"Oh hell no! Not in my truck!" He finally just turned the radio right off and I slumped back in my seat with my arms crossed and pouted.

"Fine." I would find a way to get him back but it might take time. That was ok, I had all the time in the world. I started to smirk as a plan started to form in my mind. Thinking about how I was going to get my revenge kept my mind from thinking about meeting my sister and before I knew it we were in front of a huge house. "Seriously?"

"Your uncle's a dentist, a very good one apparently." Aiden said sliding out of the truck. Before I had even moved my hand toward the door handle he was there opening the door for me. He held his hand out for me but I couldn't bring myself to put my hand in his.

"It's really happening isn't it?" I asked wistfully, frightened of what might happen. "After all this time, I'm finally going to meet my sister?"

"Yeah Pix, you are now come on, she's waiting for you." He said tugging on my hand slightly forcing me out of the truck. I followed him, pulling back slightly on his hand as he walked ahead of me dragging me up the front walk. Before we even got to the door it was flung open and a slightly younger version of me flung herself at me.

I caught her but just barely. She was a little shorter than me but that could have been the boots I was wearing. Her hair was just as red as mine but much longer and I think her eyes were probably gray like mine but I hadn't really seen her face yet. She was hugging me so tight and babbling away.

"I knew he would do it! I knew he would find you!" She cried swaying back and forth with me in her arms. "Ever since he told me about you when I was ten I asked for you for my birthday and Christmas and Easter and when I lost a tooth, you were the only thing I ever wanted and he finally brought you to me. I can't believe you're finally here!"

"Ash sweetheart, let's let Grace-Lynn and Aiden come inside and sit down." A slightly older man said. This was my uncle, his hair was gray but I recognized my mother in him. "Please, come inside and we'll talk, I'll tell you everything I promise." I looked to Aiden who nodded and took my hand then my sister took my other hand and led me inside with her.

We went into a rather formal living room and Aiden and I sat on the couch. I tried to sit in the corner but my sister wouldn't let me and she sat so close to me I thought she would end up in my lap. Now that I'd found her apparently she wasn't letting me go.

"You're here." She whispered, holding out a hand to touch my hair and then my cheek. I looked closely at her now and she really could have been my twin, not just my sister. Even our freckles looked the same. Her hair though was long and much thicker than mine would have been had I let it grow. Ash-Lynn stared at me with the same intensity that I did her and smiled when our eyes met. We both turned when our uncle, or her dad cleared his throat.

"I'm sorry." Was all he said at first. "I wanted to take you both but my wife at the time wouldn't allow it. We both assumed incorrectly that we would have more children and she was barely willing to take Ashlyn but finally relented. I tried for so long to convince her to take you as well Grace-Lynn but she just wouldn't budge.

When she found out she couldn't have any more children she sunk into a depression and raged at everyone and everything. Eventually she couldn't take life anymore and she got in her car and drove it off a cliff on the Coquihalla. The police didn't find her body for almost a month and by then they needed dental records to identify her remains.

"That was the year I told Ashlyn about you and we've been trying to find you ever since." He sighed again and rubbed his forehead. "I was told because I didn't accept you when you were little it would be harder for me to find information about you. The moment I thought I had found you the system moved you to another home and the search began again. You would think it would be easy to find one little girl in a city this size but the system is so overloaded that as soon as you were moved your case worker would become so busy it would take six months just to make an appointment with her and then you would disappear again."

"And then I aged out and the city had no records for me." I said nodding.

"Are you mad at us?" Ashlyn asked, squeezing my hand in hers.

I looked at her confused. "No, how could I be mad? I admit I thought I would be, not at you but at our uncle but I can't bring myself to be angry. I never stopped looking for you or hoping I would find you and then Aiden did and my emotions went wild. I'm so happy I couldn't be angry."

"Is Aiden your boyfriend?" Ashlyn asked smiling cheekily.

"Oh, no not really we . . . well he . . . I -"

"We are exploring a relationship but we are not dating per se." Aiden answered, winking at me. "You're sister's had a very difficult few months and we're taking anything between us very slowly."

"Oh, are you ok?" Ashlyn asked, worried.

"Yes, I think now I am ok." I answered her honestly.

CHAPTER 11

Grace-Lynn

I was having lunch with my sister. I was sitting in a restaurant on a Saturday afternoon a week after finally finding her again and I was in shock. I was also smiling like an idiot, I couldn't help myself. We had talked every night for over an hour since last Friday when Aiden had taken me to her house. Aiden himself was here with us but was sitting by the door of the restaurant acting as protection.

My sister was talking a mile a minute about all sorts of things that I couldn't keep up with. Mostly it was about school and how excited she was to be graduating this year and how I had to go to her graduation and celebrate with her and we had to get our hair done together.

Then she'd stop talking and just look at me and smile. Most of the time we were together I would do the same, just sit and watch her be happy. We had missed so much but now that I had her back I was not letting her go.

I also sat facing the door so I could see Aiden. Every so often he would look over at me and smile. At one point as I watched him he sat up straight with his gaze sharply directed outside but seconds later relaxed and sat back again.

I thought maybe he had seen D or Briggs but so far he hadn't made a move to make us leave. Ashlyn and I hung out for a little while longer then got up and walked out hand in hand. With Ash on one side of me and Aiden on the other I couldn't have been happier. Then Aiden's phone rang.

"Yeah," he said, pulling us to a stop beside him. He mmhmm'd a couple of times then swore and hung up. "Let's go. Ashlyn for now you're going with us."

"What's going on?" I asked as he pulled us to his truck.

"I'll explain on the way, I need to get you somewhere safe." He clipped as he practically threw us into the truck. Before climbing in himself he slid underneath it then within minutes was up and sitting beside me in the truck.

"Aiden, what on earth is going on?" I demanded again.

"That was Lo on the phone." He replied, his eyes everywhere as he drove. "Judy was in an accident."

"Judy?" Ashlyn asked, sitting forward to see Aiden.

"The mother of another club member." I explained to her, then turned back to Aiden. "What kind of accident?"

"She said her car lost its brakes and she lost control of it." He said, pulling into the parking lot of the hospital.

"But it's a brand new car." I exclaimed.

"I know." Aiden said tightly as he parked and we all rushed into the hospital. All the members were there waiting, Kat was sitting but Hammer, Judy's son was pacing. As soon as we walked in Lo and Axle walked over to Aiden and pulled him aside.

Seether

I was furious. Judy was off limits, as was Alana's family but D had threatened them all.

"What's going on?" I demanded as Lo and Axle pulled me aside.

"Judy is ok; she's got a broken arm and a bit of a concussion but otherwise not too bad." Lo explained, planting his hands on his hips. "The car wasn't too badly damaged and one of our guys checked it out on the scene. He said the brake line had been cut."

"What the fuck?" I whispered. I knew it had to be something like that because it was a new car and Judy was careful. She'd also had Kat check the whole thing out when she bought it and Kat was an ace mechanic.

"We think it was Little D but we don't have any witnesses. We need you to hack CCTV." Axle said quietly, his eyes watching the people around us. "We need to see who it was."

"Yeah, done," I replied nodding. "I'll do it as soon as we get back to the clubhouse."

Just then a doctor stepped into the waiting room. "Family of Judith Bennet?"

We all stood behind Hammer as he whirled on the doctor. "I'm her son."

"Mr. Bennet, your mom is going to be just fine. As we said before she has a minor concussion and a broken wrist but she should heal nicely. She is free to go home as long as there is someone there with her, just as soon as her cast is finished." The doctor said somewhat nervously, eyeing all of us gathered around Hammer.

"We'll be staying with her." Hammer replied, pulling Kat into him and hugging her tight to his chest.

The doctor gave a few more instructions about Judy's care and then left. We all agreed we would head back to the clubhouse and one of us would bring a few bags to Judy's for Hammer and Kat while they stayed there.

We all went our separate ways and Pixie and I took her sister home. I let her dad know about the trouble and to keep an eye on Ashlyn for a while and then we went home.

"Are you hungry?" I asked Pixie as we went into my room.

"No, I just ate lunch." She chuckled, turning on me smiling. She stepped towards me and placed her hands on my chest. She was wearing high heels so she was a little bit closer to my height but still much shorter than me. Before I knew what she was doing she slid one hand up around the back of my neck and stretched up on her toes, pulling me down so our lips met.

I was surprised but not so surprised that I didn't slide my hands around her waist. One of my hands slid down and cupped her ass and she gasped into my mouth and froze.

"Is that ok Pix?" Her face was still tilted up towards mine but her eyes were still closed. She seemed to think for a moment as her brow puckered then she nodded just slightly and reached up for me again.

I obliged her and kissed her again, licking at the seam of her lips until she opened her mouth and let me in. Her tongue darted out to duel with mine then she retreated and she pulled back and buried her face in my chest.

"I'm sorry I shouldn't have done that." She said, shaking her head.

"Why not? I liked it. Did you like it?" Pixie nodded yes but kept her face hidden. I tucked a finger under her chin and tipped her face up to look at me then pushed my hips into her stomach. "You feel that? I'm fucking hard as a rock. That's the first time I've had a hard on in five years that wasn't chemically induced and you did that."

She stepped back quickly, suddenly looking very unsure.

"Stop, Pix. Just because you make me hard doesn't mean I'm going to take advantage. I'll either take care of it myself or it will just go away on its own. I don't expect you to do anything about it."

"I know." She whispered nodding. "I do know that, I'm just scared that I want to do something about it but I don't think I'm ready for that."

"Ok, that's ok. I'm glad you want to do something about my hard on." I chuckled and shook my head. "But like I said, I don't expect it and I'm not going to ask for it. I am going to ask you to help me hack into CCTV to find out who cut Judy's brake line though."

"I can do that." She said smiling widely. I kissed her one more time on the lips then turned her to the computers and pushing her gently towards the chair that was now hers. "Um Aiden?"

"Yeah Pix?"

"I noticed on your calendar you've got Wednesday of last week circled. What's so important about that day?" She asked as she started typing.

"Uh, it was that day five years ago that . . ." I said trailing off. I had completely forgotten all about it.

"Oh, I'm sorry. I shouldn't have said anything." She said quickly looking horrified.

"No, it's ok. I actually forgot all about it. I guess there's been so much going on that it just slipped my mind. I think I even slept that night didn't I?"

"Well, I think you've slept just about every night for the last couple of weeks so probably." She said, shrugging and smiled. "Here, I'm in CCTV, what's the address we're looking for?"

"Judy's car was parked at the school district office all day and she said her brakes here fine this morning. That's right outside OLPH school." I said sitting beside her, letting the previous conversation slip away, as if it were that easy.

CHAPTER 12

Grace-Lynn

"We have news." Lo said the next day when we walked into this office. Sharpie, Axle and Hammer were all there and none of them looked happy. I turned to the couch where I normally sat and saw Edith there. This was strange, Edith was not normally part of these meetings but what did I really know about it?

"We've just been informed that Constable Michaels has been arrested for his part in all of this." Sharpie said when we were all comfortable.

"Pixie, what can you tell us about Matthew Briggs?" Lo asked.

"He used to meet with D and Michaels all the time, and then your guy Demon started going to meetings but never when Briggs was there. D would say that they were using Demon to get to the club." I answered as I curled up beside Edith.

"He said the club?" Axle asked pointedly. "Not a particular person in the club?"

"He mentioned that you were his step-son, Axle and that he hated you but that he was after the club. He never did say why and I was never encouraged to ask questions." I shrugged.

"Briggs is back." Lo said his gaze boring into Edith.

"We know," Aiden said sitting beside me. "That's who cut Judy's brake line, that's what we were coming to tell you."

"Fuck that fucker!" Hammer hissed angrily.

"He was hiding with D for a while after you guys left him at the hospital but he'd disappeared before I came here." I said weakly, I had told them all of this before but I wanted to make sure they understood I had nothing to do with Briggs.

"We know, it's ok Pixie." Aiden said, taking my hand in his. "So what's Briggs up to now?"

"He's been sending Edith texts from multiple burner phones, more than forty a day from the looks of it." Axle replied sighing heavily, "And he's threatened all of the women in those texts including Judy and Alana's parents. He did leave you out of it though Pixie."

"He really didn't know about me." I shrugged sheepishly. "I didn't like him so the few times we were both at the house at the same time I left right away and stayed out of his way."

"Smart." Edith murmured, patting my knee. "Briggs is not a nice man."

"We need to keep an eye on everyone. Brooke is about to go into the hospital to have the baby and Kat is about ready to pop, too." Axle said, scratching the back of his head. "I don't like staying all the way out here in case something happens and we have to hurry to the hospital."

"I agree." Lo said, sighing heavily. "We'll get you guys set up at the apartment in town."

"You have an apartment in town?" I asked, frowning.

"Yeah we keep a condo in town for different situations. We usually only use it for people visiting when we don't have space here at the clubhouse but it comes in handy." Aiden said, putting an arm around my shoulder.

"David!" We all heard Brooke scream from the main room of the clubhouse and we all rushed out in a hurry. She stood in the middle of the room in a puddle of water.

"Is that what I think it is?" Axle demanded.

"Well I didn't pee myself." Brooke retorted snarkily. Brooke was snarky? "Oh shit!" she cried and clutched her stomach.

"Angel baby let's get you to the hospital." Axle rushed forward and lifted her into his arms.

"No shit Sherlock!" Brooke exclaimed, biting her lip as another contraction hit her.

"Isn't she early?" I asked Aiden as Axle rushed his fiancé out of the building.

"Only by like a few days or something, nothing serious." He replied shrugging. "We'll meet you at the hospital!" He called as we started walking after them, each of us pulling on coats.

"Hey, what's going on?" Kat asked waddling into the room.

"Brooke's in labour." Hammer said, handing her a jacket. "Let's go you can't stay here alone and I wouldn't miss seeing Axle freak out for anything."

"You're so mean." Kat said smiling as she let Hammer help her into her coat. She was so big that it wouldn't close in front and her ankles looked painfully swollen.

"We'll stay behind and I'll keep an eye on Edith." Sharpie called to us as we left.

We all walked out of the clubhouse much more slowly than Axle had and started to climb into trucks when gunshots started firing.

"No!" Kat cried and we all turned to find her held in front of

Briggs as he held a gun to her temple.

"Shut up!" He yelled at her as he tried to pull her back but pulled her off balance instead and she fell back against him, knocking him against the wall of the building. Shots were continually fired from the street and the guys were all yelling to stay down but Hammer was running to Kat, trying to get her to safety.

When Briggs had regained his balance he raised his gun again and started shooting from behind us towards the street. I don't know if he was trying to hit us or whoever the other person shooting was.

Whatever he was going for he managed to hit the passenger of the vehicle and we heard a shout of pain, then a pause in the shooting and one more shot that found its home in Brigg's chest, pushing him back again against the wall of the clubhouse where he slumped and didn't move.

"Kat!" Hammer cried, holding her sitting in his lap. When I took a closer look I saw blood dripping from her shoulder and realized she had been hit by a bullet.

Seether

We all shook out of our shock at the same time and rushed over to Hammer and Kat as the car screeched away up the road away from us. He looked up at us pleadingly as she sat in his lap limply.

"Come on," Lo said, smacking Hammer on the back of the head. "We've got to get her to the hospital. I'll call Sharpie on the way and get him to take care of Briggs."

Lo leaned down and picked Kat up and held her until Hammer was up and able to take her from him. We all rushed over to the SUV the club had and piled in so we could help Hammer keep an eye on Kat while Lo drove. We got to the hospital in record time and Pixie ran inside to get help.

Between waiting to hear about Brooke and her baby and Kat and her babies and her wound we were all wound pretty tight. Hammer was with us since Kat had been rushed into surgery for her gunshot wound and he was once again pacing the floor. I sat in a chair with my head back against the wall and Pixie cuddled against my chest. Alana had arrived not too long after we got to the hospital and said she had taken Judy over to her mom and dad's house.

Hammer barely grunted thanks and kept pacing. Now Alana sat in a chair with Lo much like Pixie was with me and we waited. We kept waiting until a doctor came into the room and looked around.

"Is the family of Katherine Bishop here?"

"Yes," Hammer said, stepping to the doctor. "I'm her fiancé."

"Is there family here that is next of kin?"

"What do you need next of kin for?" Hammer demanded angrily. "She can't be dead! She only had a gunshot wound in her shoulder! What about the babies?"

"Oh no," the doctor immediately backtracked. "No, Ms. Bishop is fine; she's resting comfortably in a room on the maternity floor. Are you the father of her babies?"

"Did I not just say I was her fiancé?" Hammer demanded getting even angrier.

"I'm sorry; when she came in we had very little information. Ms. Bishop came through the surgery on her shoulder wonderfully with no problems. During the surgery however the babies began to show signs of distress so we had to deliver them by emergency C-section. That's why mother is in the maternity ward, she's sharing a room with a Brooke Crosbie? The babies, one girl and two boys, are in the Special Care Nursery for observation just because they are a bit early. All three appear to be healthy and stable . . . um, congratulations, and sorry for the misunderstanding."

"Idiot," Hammer muttered, shaking his head. "Hey, what's the room number?"

"310 west," The doctor called back, hurrying away as he was paged. Hammer rushed over to the elevator and pushed the button for the 3rd floor. We followed him but the elevator was moving too slowly for him and he rushed over to the stairs. We all waited for the elevator though as we weren't in quite the same rush that Hammer was.

CHAPTER 13

Grace-Lynn

When we knocked on the door of the room Brooke and Kat were sharing we found Hammer cuddled up with a sleeping Kat and Brooke breast feeding her new daughter with Axle watching impatiently.

"Seriously Brooke, hurry up I want her back." Axle said rushing Brooke who just looked up at him like he was nuts.

"I don't think Brooke has any control over that." Alana said laughing at Axle. "How are you feeling sweetie?"

"Tired," Brooke replied smiling softly. She looked just like the Angel Axle claimed she was. "But so great. Imogen Adeline, she's so perfect." Axle shooed us away and sat on the bed, wrapping his arm around his woman and child.

"You only get to hold her when I'm not around, woman." Axle said sternly, pointing at Alana who stuck her tongue out at him and laughed. Then he looked at Lo and raised an eyebrow. "She laughs but I'm completely serious."

"I know you are brother." Lo chuckled, shaking his head, then looked over to where Kat was blinking slowly and Hammer was whispering in her ear. "How's your sister?"

"Banged up and sore, tired but ok. Confused, I think, the doctors didn't explain it all to her." Axle said, shaking his head disgustedly. "That's probably what Hammer's doing now if that expression on her face is any indication."

"She was probably too out of it for them to tell her." Alana said, shrugging.

"Go see them." Kat said, suddenly pushing at Hammer's shoulder. "Please Sam; go see our babies so I know they're ok."

"Come on Hammer, I'll go with you." Alana said, patting Kat's foot under her blanket. "At least those babies I'll get a chance to hold." She said teasing Axle.

"Don't count on it!" He called to her as she left the room with Hammer.

"I'll be up in a minute." Lo said as he watched her go. "How did Briggs get on our property?"

"Fuck if I know man." Axle said, shaking his head. "Seether, you check the cameras?"

"Haven't had a chance," Aiden replied, also shaking his head. "We followed you out here minutes after you left. As soon as all the baby craze has settled a bit we'll go back and take a look, I'll call or text you all and let you know what I find."

"Sounds good brother," Lo said then left the room.

When little Imogen was finished with her mommy Brooke passed the baby to her daddy who burped her and cuddled against his chest. Brooke watched them together with a soft look in her eyes then looked over at Kat who was also watching her brother with his daughter.

"Don't worry Kat," Brooke said quietly. "You'll have your babies here with you soon." Kat nodded with wet eyes then smiled slightly.

"Have you thought of names?" I asked her, perching on the edge of her bed.

"We had thought if the baby was a boy he would be Alex David after Axle, and if it was a girl she would be Lexi Judith but now we've got two boys and one girl and I don't know what we're going to do." Kat laughed softly then winced when her shoulder jarred a little.

"Well, you all better get home really soon because I can't wait to meet all your little ones." I said patting her knee and standing as Aiden stepped towards us. "I'm not working and I've got lots of free time so you make sure you let me know if you need help rocking babies or changing diapers."

"I'll do that." Kat chuckled then waved as we left the room. We met Lo and Alana at the truck a few minutes later and we stopped at a restaurant on our way home for supper. It wasn't quite that late in the day but none of us wanted to go home and cook and since Alana's boys were with her parents she didn't have to rush home.

It suddenly struck me that Aiden and I had never talked about babies. I mean really why would we, after all that we were dealing with anyway we didn't need to bring babies into it and we hadn't known each other that long. Still, after spending the day at the hospital surrounded by baby fever it made me wonder.

Seether

I was sitting at my computer going over the security cameras of the compound when Pixie came out of the bathroom drying her hair with a towel, steam following her. I looked up at her and smiled and felt my cock jump at seeing her dressed in one of my t-shirts. That seemed to be all she wanted to wear to bed anymore and I fucking loved it. Her question though shocked the hell out of me.

"Do you want kids?"

"What?" My head snapped back in surprise and I think the crack of my voice scared her.

"Never mind," She said quickly shaking her head, "It was a stupid question."

"Pixie stop, it wasn't a stupid question it just took me by surprise. Honestly I hadn't thought about kids before. Do you want kids?"

She shrugged almost sullenly. "I think so? I don't know really. I always just thought I would have kids but I have never dated anyone who I wanted to have kids with before."

"Would you want to have kids with me?" I asked, not really sure what I wanted to hear.

"If I were going to have kids with anyone then yes I would want that person to be you." She said easily and I was absolutely relieved.

"Can I ask you something?"

"Didn't you just ask me something?" She smiled and shrugged.

"Were you a virgin when D raped you?"

Pixie was surprised by the question but she didn't run away from it either. "No, I'd only had one partner before that and while the sex was nothing spectacular, at least I don't think it was, it was comfortable and enjoyable."

I nodded, not sure what to say to that so I said nothing, just smiled and turned back to the computer and that's when I saw Briggs on my screen. He was just walking onto the compound, looking around for anyone who might be around.

I followed him from camera feed to camera feed until he came to a stop at the back of the building on the garage side where we kept our bikes in the winter and some of the cars and bikes we worked on in the shop. Briggs pulled a back pack off his shoulders and started pulling things out of it.

"What does he have?" Pixie asked as she stood behind me, her hand on my shoulder.

"I don't know but it can't –" and that's when it happened. The screen playing the camera feed in real time flashed and the world around me flew back in time. My brain automatically sent me back five years to the day I sat up in a blind in Afghanistan watching my teammates being blown to hell.

"Aiden!" Pixie screamed as the ground shook around us and my ears rang as I looked up at her and saw the eyes of the woman in that hut, only it was Pixie's face. "Aiden please, we have to go, Aiden we have to get out of here!"

Finally I shook myself out of the stupor the blast had shoved me into and I jumped up, grabbing my phone off the charger and ran out to the parking lot, calling 911 as I ran.

When we got outside I realized Pixie was still only wearing my t-shirt and no shoes so I put her in my truck and drove it across to the far side of the lot and left it running with the heater on. Then I ran back to the back of the building to see what the damage was.

Luckily the blast hadn't erupted in fire but had blown a huge hole in the wall and the flying debris had knocked out quite a few of the bikes stored inside. When Lo had built the clubhouse he had smartly put the private rooms on one side of the main room and the shop and garage on the other side. The blast was big enough that we felt it in our room but not big enough to actually damage anything in the rooms or hurt anyone.

Soon, the two prospects who were staying at the compound came running over to join me, looking inside what was our garage.

"Fuck." One of them said, shaking his head in disbelief while the other one nodded in agreement. These two were like tweedle dee and tweedle dum. It wasn't long before an ambulance, fire truck and police car arrived and activity started making me dizzy. I walked slowly to my truck and climbed into to wait for Lo to arrive and the police to start asking questions.

CHAPTER 14

Grace-Lynn

I don't know what happened to Aiden when that bomb went off but it looked like he had completely left me in that room. Now it was three days later and Brooke was home with her baby and was staying at her own house with Axle and Aiden was still not back to himself.

Kat was still at the hospital and Hammer was staying with her and the babies. Aiden and I were staying at the condo while the clubhouse was being repaired and every night he slept, or didn't sleep on the couch. I was starting to get worried that he was reverting back to the Aiden I first met when I first came to the clubhouse and it scared me.

Right now we were in the living room of Alana's ranch house on the other side of the property from the clubhouse and she was losing her mind on Lo. I couldn't say I blamed her; the kids weren't home when the bomb went off but they sure as hell could have been.

"You said we were safe here!" She screamed, getting right in his face. "You promised! You said you would protect us!"

"Alana!" Lo hollered in her face to get her attention. She froze and stared at him then broke down and would have slumped to the floor if he hadn't caught her. "You are safe, I did promise you would be safe and I meant it. I will not let anything happen to you or the kids or the babies or anyone else. I swear it to you."

He picked her up as she nodded, sobbing into his chest and sat in his arm chair with her in his lap.

"It was Briggs who set the bomb." Aiden said stonily, staring at a spot on the floor. "He's dead, now we just have to find D."

"We just heard the other day that Constable Michaels was found in his cell hanging from the ceiling." Sharpie said from the fireplace across the room. "We haven't been told yet if it was actually suicide, or if he was murdered but he's dead as well."

"So, it really is just D that we have to find." Axle mumbled patting Imogen's back and she slept against his chest. "Pixie would any of D's guys continue his shit if he died? Do any of them have the balls to take over?"

"No," I said, shaking my head. "All D's guys are just along for the ride. They're followers not leaders and none of them are smart enough to keep his little enterprise going. They're there for the free drugs and women."

"Well that's something." Axle sighed heavily.

"Cut the head off the snake and the tail slithers away." Lo agreed. We all sat for a little while longer then everyone started to disperse and go their separate ways.

"Take me home?" I whispered to Aiden who nodded and stood, walking out of the house without saying a word.

The drive back to the condo was also silent and he seemed to brood the whole way. When we got back to the condo he checked to make sure all the windows and doors were locked then slumped on the couch and stared at the tv even though he hadn't turned it on.

"Are you going to come to bed?"

"No," He answered but otherwise ignored me.

"Well, at least I got a verbal rejection that time." I said sighing as I walked towards the bedroom.

"What?"

"What? You've been ignoring me for three days. That's the first word you've said to me. Usually when I ask you something you either ignore me or look right through me. So thank you for finally speaking to me." I shrugged and turned back heading to the bedroom again.

"What do you want from me?" He demanded pushing himself off of the couch.

"I want my friend back!" I yelled at him getting angry. "I don't know what I did to make you disappear like this but I want you back!"

"You didn't do anything." He muttered, shaking his head then dropping his chin to his chest and gripping his hair in his hands. "You didn't do a fucking thing."

"Then what is going on?"

"It's nothing–"

"It's not nothing! One minute you're laughing and talking with me then the world explodes and you're a totally different person! I want to know what is going on."

"It was you!" he hollered, turning on me. "The flash from that blast took me back five years and it was your face I saw in the scope of my rifle! Not that other woman! You! Every damn time I close my eyes I see you lying dead on the dirt floor of that damn fucking hut! Are you happy? Now you fucking know!"

Aiden seemed to deflate in front of me as he sank to the carpet, his face in his hands and sobbing.

"Oh Aiden, baby," I whispered kneeling beside him and wrapping him in my arms. "It's not me in that hut, it wasn't me and I'm right here and I'm alive and well." I kissed his temple and pulled his hands from his face. "Come on, I'll show you."

Seether

I didn't know what Pixie had planned but when she pulled my hands from my face and replaced them with hers I wasn't sure I cared. She leaned towards me and pressed her lips to mine opening her mouth over mine and pushing her tongue inside. She licked over my tongue making me drag in a sharp breath. God she tasted better than I remembered.

Slowly so I didn't scare her I took over the kiss, pushing my hands into her short hair and pulled her hard against me. She moaned into my mouth and tilted her head, giving me better access to her. I pulled away and trailed kisses down her throat and sucked on her pulse at the base of her throat.

"Pixie," I whispered as she whimpered and held me to her.

"Aiden, I want you," She whispered, lifting my mouth back to hers. "Please make love to me." She begged a split second before she sealed her lips over mine.

I groaned and pulled back from her breathing hard.

"Are you sure Pixie?"

"I'm sure I love you Aiden. I'm sure I want you to be my first real lover. I'm sure I want you forever and I'm sure you will never hurt me. Please Aiden."

My breath caught in my chest as she said it and I stared deep into her clear gray eyes that were slowly being swallowed by her pupils as they dilated with desire. I kissed her again and stood, lifting her with me then carried her to the room she was using then set her on her feet beside the bed.

"Fuck Pixie, I'm not prepared for this, I love you and I want to make love to you but I don't have a condom, I need to protect you." I said shaking my head and holding her at arms-length.

"Aiden, you love me?"

"Yeah Pix, I fucking love you with everything that I am."

"Aiden you haven't had sex in over five years, I'm pretty sure you don't have any diseases, and I was checked after . . . well after, and I just finished my period two days ago so it's too soon for me to get pregnant. Aiden, just this once, do we need a condom?"

She was gazing up at me with so much love in her eyes I wanted to just forget all about the condom but I had to be sure.

"Pixie, are you sure? We can wait."

"No Aiden, I cannot wait. I want you now. I'm very sure."

"This isn't going to take very long Pixie, it's been too long for me and I love you too fucking much. It's going to be really fast."

"Fast, slow I don't care, I just want you." She breathed and started pulling my shirt up my chest.

She was wearing a button up blouse and slowly I undid each button then bent and kissed each little bit of skin I exposed. Soon I was pushing the shirt off her shoulders and dropping it to the floor at our feet.

I reached behind my head and pulled my shirt off and tossed it across the room, not caring where it fell. I looked down at Pixie and cupped my hands around her bare shoulders then slid them up to cup her jaw.

I rubbed my thumbs over her bottom lip then kissed her deeply and her nails raked over my pecs and down my abs. She bent her head to the side and I kissed down the side of her neck and pulled her bra strap off her shoulder with my teeth. She gasped as I dragged my teeth across her sensitive skin and kissed the tender flesh kneeling in front of her pulling her bra down around her waist and undoing the clasp at the back.

Pixie's breasts were small but full and high. Her nipples were the same soft brown as the freckles that covered her milky skin. I sucked softly on the skin just below her breast bone then trailed my tongue up between her breasts and kissed each one. I pushed my hands up from her waist and molded her breasts together and sucked hard on each of her nipples, worshiping each in turn.

She moaned and pulled my hair but didn't drag me away from my adoration of her. Slowly I slipped my hand down to the waistband of her pants and undid the button and zipper. So slowly I dragged the fly of her jeans down then pushed at the waistband until they hung off her hips. I moved into her on my knees pushing her back to sit on the edge of the bed then pulled her jeans and panties off her legs.

Pixie sat in front of me in her perfection of creamy, satiny skin covered in little beauty marks. I leaned forward and kissed her lips, standing from my knees and wrapping my arm around her waist to lift her up to the head of the bed then settled just to the side of her so we were chest to chest but I wasn't laying on her or crowding her.

"Aiden," She moaned when my hand cupped her breast again then trailed lightly, tickling her as I went to cup her sex.

Her hips arched slightly under my palm as my fingers slid through her soft, soaking lips to her entrance. I wanted to push a finger inside her but didn't dare until she was completely ready. I didn't want to scare her and I really wanted to taste her.

"Baby," I kissed her lightly on the lips then skimmed my mouth down her body until I hovered just above her sweetness. "I'm gonna taste you baby ... that ok with you?"

"Mmmm, Aiden..." She whispered then arched her hips off the bed.

I smiled wickedly up at her and covered her pussy with my mouth, licking inside her. She arched her back and cried out as I dragged my tongue from her center to her clit and flicked my tongue over her then sucked her into my mouth.

Slowly as I sucked her I slid a finger inside her and pumped it in and out gently. She moaned again undulating her hips with my movements. Soon I added another finger and crooked them as I pumped so they rubbed her g-spot.

As the muscles of her thighs started to quiver I sped my thrusts and suck harder on her clit until she came in my mouth and over my hand.

I rubbed her and licked her through her orgasm until her breathing was almost back to normal, then I began to crawl up her body undoing my pants and pushing them down my legs.

By the time I was hovering over her so I could kiss her and share her taste on my tongue my pants and underwear were around my ankles. I lifted a knee, spreading her legs more and pulling one foot free.

She whimpered and it wasn't the sound of a woman who was enjoying herself so I rolled over onto my back dragging her across my chest.

"Oh..." She gasped, her eyes wide.

"You ok?" I asked, cupping her cheek. She nodded and sat up slightly to look down at me then looked down my chest to where she was sitting on my stomach, just above my cock. "If you want to stop we will stop right now."

She shook her head frantically. "No, I don't want to stop ... I just ... it was just a second, I'm fine now, I want to keep going."

"Ok, wrap your hand around me and guide me into you." I said smoothing my fingers over her cheek, my other hand resting on her thigh. She did as I said and lined me up to her opening then moaned.

"Aiden, I think you're too big . . . " She whimpered then slowly slid down my length gasping.

"Mmmm, baby that's something every guy wants to hear but I promise you I'll fit." I chuckled then groaned deep in my throat as I slid even deeper inside her. Yes I was thick but I was also long and I wasn't sure she would get all of me inside her but she did and I could feel her warm ass against my thighs as she settled over me. Her hands curled into my chest as she threw her head back and gasped.

"Oh God!"

"No baby, just Aiden." I said and she snorted a laugh. "Ride me baby, make yourself feel good."

"I can't Aiden, I don't know how." She almost wailed the frustration clear on her face. "Oohhh, I'm so full . . ."

"Lift up a little . . . now settle down again . . . uuhhnnnn and up . . . and down . . . fuck that's it baby . . ." Pixie followed my directions and soon found her rhythm until I couldn't take it anymore and I had to take over.

I grasped her hips tight in my hands and pumped up into her hard as she thrust down against me.

Three, four, five more thrusts and she cried out and her pussy clamped around me and milked my cock as I came harder than I remember ever coming in any history let alone recent history.

Pixie fell against my chest, panting and kissing my throat, her inner muscles still twitching against my dick.

I rolled her to the side but didn't pull out of her completely and kissed her lips gently, sipping from her as she sighed and relaxed against me.

"I love you Grace-Lynn." I whispered to her, kissing her lips as she smiled and opened her eyes to gaze into mine.

"I love you Aiden. I want you forever. Thank you for giving me this back." She said closing her eyes and drifting into sleep.

CHAPTER 15

Seether

I woke up the next morning after the greatest sleep I'd ever have with the feel of something soft and wet and warm around my very hard and aching cock. Lifting the covers I looked down to find Pixie with her mouth around me.

"Oh God Pixie . . . fuck . . ." I moaned and panted.

"Not God baby, just your Pixie." I chuckled as she repeated my words from the night before. She licked from the base of me to the tip and swirled her tongue around the head of my cock as she pumped her saliva over me with her hand.

Pixie lowered her mouth over me until I could feel the back of her throat and she swallowed then sucked hard, hollowing her cheeks as she pulled me out of her mouth.

I started to feel that tickle at the base of my spine and my balls begin to pull up and I knew I was about to cum.

"Uuhnnn, baby stop . . ." I reached down to pull her up but she swatted my hands away and kept sucking on me. "Baby, I'm gonna come, let go . . ."

"No." She said then continued sucking and licking, fondling my balls with one hand as the other pumped opposite her mouth.

"Fuck . . . baby, I'm . . ." that was all the warning she got before I was shooting my cum down her throat. She swallowed it all then licked my cock clean and kissed her way up my body until she was lying over my chest. "You're fucking amazing." I panted when I had caught my breath enough to talk.

She chuckled over me as she drew little circles with her finger tips around my nipple. "You're welcome."

I rubbed my hands lazily up and down her back only now realizing she was wearing a shirt. "What's this?" I asked, pulling at it.

"I had to pee; I grabbed your shirt on my way to the bathroom." She said.

"Mmm, I like you in my shirts." I replied sighing contentedly but I knew we had to have a conversation about last night . . . and this morning. "How are you feeling?"

"Fine, good," She replied shrugging a little.

"Seriously Pixie, are you ok with last night?"

"Yeah, I am. I was a little freaked out when I woke up but then I remembered us and the fear left."

I could feel her tense a bit as she spoke but I didn't move or change my breathing, anything that would make her think I was upset about her being scared when she woke up.

My heart rate was already through the roof still from that blow job so that wouldn't give anything away.

"I know you would never hurt me but it's also completely irrational."

"No it's not Pixie. It's not irrational at all. You suffered trauma, what he did to you –"

"Not here," She interrupted me sitting up and straddling my hips, "I don't want to talk about him or that here in our bed.

What we do here is beautiful and perfect and I don't want him or that clouding this. There will be times when I let it into my head and I will get scared but in my heart it is only you and me here."

I levered up until I was sitting under her, my chest brushing her soft breasts. I cupped her cheeks and kissed her deeply.

Grace-Lynn

As Aiden kissed me I started to get more and more excited. Giving him a blow job had already excited me but I had been content to let him have that and not ask for reciprocation. But now as he kissed me and his chest teased my hard nipples and I felt his cock harden under my ass I couldn't help myself.

I started grinding my pussy against him as the ache between my legs grew. I could feel my own fluids dripping down the insides of my thighs and thought I must be soaking Aiden.

"Baby, are you sore?" He whispered, pushing my shirt up over my head. I shook my head no as his hands cupped and massaged my breasts and I closed my eyes and rolled my head back as he plumped them then pinched and rolled my nipples between his fingers.

He alternated between pinching the nipple and squeezing my entire breast in his big hands and I thought I was going to cum just from that.

Then he pushed one hand up behind my head and pulled me down and kissed me hard, pushing his tongue in my mouth and licking the roof then sucked my tongue into his mouth. He nipped my lips with his teeth then soothed them with little licks and kisses. He continued this as his other hand slid down between us and started to rub and swirl around my clit, making me grind against him harder trying to relieve the ache.

"Lift up baby," He whispered then reached between my legs and pulled his cock up and notched it into my opening and held it there. "Whenever you're ready baby, take it as slow or as fast as you want."

I stared into his eyes, feeling myself almost drown in their green depths then reached down to pull his hand from between us and sank onto him, feeling him fill me up until I could feel him against my cervix. We groaned together as I lifted up again then dropped down, squeezing him with my inner muscles as I went.

"Wait baby, I can't get any leverage like this." He wrapped his arm around my hips and pushed us to the edge of the bed then stood, still inside me and walked us to the wall each step rubbing my clit and bringing me closer and closer to orgasm. I cried out when my back touched the wall and he thrust up into me. "Hold tight baby."

I wrapped my legs around his waist and dug my nails into his shoulders as his hands slid around to grasp my ass cheeks. He spread them and dug his fingers into the crease of my ass and thrust harder and harder, each one rubbing my clit bringing me to the brink of explosion.

I dropped my head back against the wall with a thump and clenched my legs trying to pull him deeper, and then as I shattered I bit into his chest and screamed.

He thrust twice more then emptied his cum into me and relaxed, pushing me into the wall. Slowly he let my legs drop from around his waist and I licked and kissed his chest, soothing the bit mark. He held me until he was sure I was steady on my feet then tipped my chin up and kissed me hard on the mouth.

"I'll get a shower going." Aiden said, still breathing heavily. "Can't have Hammer and Kat find us like this when they bring the babies home."

A couple hours later we were sitting on the couch watching a movie when Hammer texted that they were in the parking garage and needed help with the babies. He could carry two of the car seats at a time but Kat couldn't carry the other one. Aiden rushed down to help them and a few minutes later led them into the apartment.

"Kat," I exclaimed, seeing how exhausted but happy she was. "Are you hungry or tired?"

"Both." She replied chuckling then let Hammer situate her on the couch leaning against the arm and stacked pillows all around her. I watched him dote on her until she smiled up at him and patted his cheek. He kissed her lips then left to have a shower.

"How about I make you something to eat since I'm a better cook than a babysitter." Aiden said escaping before he was roped into baby duty. Kat and I chuckled at his retreating back and then looked down at her three babies lined up in their car seats in front of her.

"Can you pass me Alex please? He's the one in the blue, I didn't get a chance to feed him before we left the hospital and I'm sure he's gonna get fussy soon." Kat asked, pointing to one of the babies.

"You did name one Alex." I said, gently lifting the little bundle and handing him to her.

"Yeah, Alex David, the one in green is Logan Samuel and our little girl is Aiden Judith but we'll call her AJ." She replied wincing as her little man latched onto her nipple to eat. "Fuck that hurts."

"I cannot even begin to imagine." I laughed as I took little AJ out of her carrier.

I was holding her and cooing at her when Aiden came back into the room with a tray full of food. He placed it on the coffee table within Kat's reach then looked at me apprehensively. Before he could shove his hands in his pockets I handed the baby to him.

"Oh no –" he said holding his hands up palms out.

"Don't be silly, just put one hand under her head and the other under her bum." I said not giving him a choice. "With hands as big as yours one of them will completely support her."

Aiden took the baby and looked down at her sleeping scrunchy little face. Then he slowly and carefully walked over to the arm chair across from the couch and sat, moving AJ to the crook of his arm.

As tiny as she was, with her head at his elbow her feet barely reached his wrist. I watched as he brushed her cheek with his fingertip and smile when she opened her mouth and yawned. He wrapped her tiny hand around his giant finger then looked up at me with so much love in his eyes.

I jumped a bit when Hammer walked up behind me and put a hand on my shoulder. Touching a finger to his lips he nodded at Kat sleeping on the couch, her boob hanging out and Alex out cold on her lap. I smiled and took the baby while Hammer lifted Kat and carried her to bed. I burped the baby then put him in his car seat to sleep and carried the food Aiden had made back to the kitchen. Luckily he had made sandwiches so it was just a matter of wrapping them up and putting them in the fridge for later.

I jumped again when his arms slid around me from behind and he kissed the crook between my neck and shoulder.

"I want one of those." He whispered. "I want one with bright red hair and covered in freckles, I want a sweet little girl with a fiery temper like I saw last night, I want her to have flashing gray eyes and delicate pixie features. I want one as tough and beautiful as her mama."

I turned in his arms and smiled up at him, looping my arms

around his neck and played with the hair hanging down over his nape. "I want a little boy who's long and lanky. I want a little boy with messy blond hair and deep green eyes. I want a little boy who's got a big heart and who's so sensitive and smart he wants to be everyone's protector and hero. I want a mini you."

Aiden kissed me deeply, running his hands up my sides, flexing his fingers into my back.

"Hey, no nookie while you're babysitting!" Hammer said walking into the kitchen. "You got those sandwiches still? I'm starving and hospital food sucks."

We laughed and handed him the plate of now wrapped sandwiches and watched him tear into them as one of the babies started to fuss in the other room.

"I'll get them." I said and rushed out.

CHAPTER 16

Seether

I watched Pixie run out of the kitchen, smiling to myself then looked over to find Hammer staring at me.

"Congratulations." He said around the huge bite of sandwich in his mouth.

"I'm pretty sure I should be telling you that." I chuckled, shaking my head.

"Yeah, accepted but congratulations for finding your happily ever after. Yours came a little harder than most." I nodded at his words.

"Yeah, I love her man; she's mine no matter what." I agreed then took one of the sandwiches I had made earlier. "I know she loves me but she is still pretty skittish and I don't blame her. I just need a plan to keep her here with me in the moment and not drifting back to Christmas."

"KISS." Hammer replied.

"What?"

"Keep it simple, stupid. It doesn't have to be a grand plan, it needs to be a simple plan and it involves one thing, love her." Hammer said, finishing off his sandwich.

"Yeah," I agreed and let his words roll around in my head.

Grace-Lynn

Kat and Hammer and their babies had been home for a couple of weeks now and we were all starting to feel a little cramped. Aiden and I agreed that it made more sense for us to find somewhere else to live than make Kat and Hammer move their family.

I thought we would just look for a little apartment close to them so I could still help with the babies. One with an extra room for all of Aiden's computers since I knew he'd been missing them since we had left them at the clubhouse.

The wall in the garage at the clubhouse had been repaired but none of us were ready to go back there to stay. Lo stayed there at night but only because it was close to Alana and the kids and they refused to live together until they were married.

I was wrong, though. The house that Aiden brought me to was much larger than I had imagined.

"What is this?" I demanded standing on the sidewalk in front of the house. "I thought we were looking at renting an apartment?"

"Why rent when we can buy?" he shrugged and walked up to the front door. The realtor was already waiting inside so we stepped in and looked around. The first room off the entrance was a large living room that was full of light from the big bow window. "What do you think?"

"I think I can't afford a house." I replied looking around and already feeling myself falling in love with the hardwood floors and medallion on the ceiling.

"No, but I can." He said, shrugging again. "I can actually afford to pay cash for this house. I really like it but we won't buy it if you don't want it."

"That's crazy, how am I going to pay you back for this?"

"Pixie, don't be ridiculous, this would be our home, you wouldn't pay me back for anything." I stared up at him dumbfounded, not sure how I felt about this. "Come on, let's see the rest of the house, if you love it then we'll buy it if you don't then we won't, simple as that."

"Right, so simple." I said motioning for him to lead us through the house.

I did fall in love with it. The house was perfect and I almost started crying when I realized that I could never be happy there if I wasn't helping pay for it. It had three bedrooms upstairs and an office downstairs off the living room.

The eatin kitchen was spacious and bright and I could totally see us having a family here. The yard was big but not huge and already had a swing set.

"Well, do you love it?" Aiden asked as we stood in the master bedroom. I shook my head no as tears started to gather in my eyes. "Do you even like it?"

I sobbed as I turned away from him, unsure how to explain what I was feeling.

"Pixie, what's wrong. Tell me how I can fix this. If it's the house we certainly don't have to buy this one, do you want a bigger one? A smaller one? What is it?"

"It's not the house Aiden." I cried, throwing my hands in the air. "I do love the house, but I can't let you buy it."

"What? Why not?"

"Because then it would be yours, not ours. I don't want that." I said, shaking my head, turning to walk out of the house.

"Wait Pixie, stop." He grabbed my hand and pulled me back into his chest. "Listen to me, please. I love you, if that means I have to buy a two hundred thousand dollar house to show you that then I will do it. You do contribute to this house; you will contribute to this house. Just because it's not with money doesn't mean you won't. You will make this house a home for me and you and our future family. You don't have to put money forward in order for you to contribute."

I shook my head still crying, "No I –"

"Stop it." He pulled me out of the house telling the realtor we would be buying the house but we had a stop to make first.

He put me in his truck and drove me down town all the while telling me how perfect the house was. It was only just around the corner from Brooke's house and it was two blocks from the condo we were currently staying in so we were still close to Kat, Hammer and their babies.

"Did you hear me say Brooke's house?" He asked at one point. "That's right, she bought it and she and Axle live there together. Do you think he gets all upset about not helping to buy it?"

"Stop it." I demanded shaking my head again.

"No." He replied and continued to tell me all about this amazing house. That is until he pulled his truck into the parking lot of a bank and parked. "Let's go." He said climbing out.

"What? No Aiden, just tell me what is going on." I said frustrated.

"No, you obviously think this is important so let me show you just how important money really is to me." He said and stomped off into the bank. I sighed and followed him in, just in time to hear the bank manager address him by name.

"Mr. Morgan, welcome back." The other man said, shaking

Aiden's hand. "Please come into my office." Aiden looked over at me as I frowned and held his hand out to me. I took it and let him lead me into the manager's office.

"Pixie this is Jeff Edwards, he's the bank manager and he handles my finances personally."

"But I thought Butch was the club's accountant." I said frowning as we sat in front of Mr. Edwards' desk.

"He is but I like to keep my money separate from the clubs." Aiden shrugged. "Jeff, can you pull up my accounts please? Pixie here doesn't believe that I can afford to buy a house for her."

"No, that's not –"

"Shh Pixie, let the man do his job." Mr. Edwards laughed and started typing on his computer.

"All right," he said, turning his monitor towards us. "This figure here is the amount that Mr. Morgan has in his savings account." I felt my eyes bug out of my head when I saw that there were six numbers after the 2 and before the decimal. "And this figure here is how much Mr. Morgan's investments add up to."

I didn't even look at that one, I didn't care. Aiden was sitting beside me slumped in his chair watching me.

"If you want to contribute money to our household fine, I won't stop you if that's what you need to feel like you aren't taking a free ride. I completely understand the need to work hard for what you have. But I feel the need to buy you a home that is safe and comfortable. I didn't bring you here to throw my money in your face because to me all of that means nothing. I brought you here to show you it doesn't matter to me. I brought you here to show you that all of that," he pointed to the computer screen, "Is as much yours as it is mine."

"No –"

"Yes Pix. What's mine is yours and what's yours is mine, that's it." I looked up at him, tears filling my eyes and over flowing down my cheeks. Aiden reached up and brushed the tears from my face then turned to Jeff. "I want you to add Pixie's name to my accounts. I want her to have complete access to everything."

"Aiden no –"

"Pixie stop, I love you and I will give you everything and you can't stop me." Aiden turned back to Jeff and told him to write up the sale for the house, that he would have to realtor contact the bank with the information and as well as add me to his accounts.

Mr. Edwards nodded and got right to work as we walked out of the bank, Aiden dragging me behind him.

When we got back to the condo I went straight to our room and closed the door, leaving Aiden in the living room with Hammer and Kat. I didn't know what to do. I didn't want Aiden's money, I didn't want to feel like I owed him, I wanted to be an equal partner in our life. I was so confused.

"Come in," I said when there was a knock on the door. Kat peaked her head through then stepped inside and closed the door behind her.

"So, you finally learned what Seether's secret was hey?" She asked sitting on the bed beside me.

"Not much of a secret if everyone knows about it." I chuckled wetly. She shrugged and smiled. "I don't know what to do. He wants to buy a house but he won't let me help pay for it."

"What's wrong with that? He has the means, why not let him?"

"I can't, if we're partners and we're together then I should be helping shouldn't I?"

"Can't you help in other ways?" Kat asked, rubbing my back. "Do you have to help financially?"

"He said the same thing."

"He's a man who knows his own mind, and he should he's spent a lot of time alone in there." She sighed and turned to face me. "Look, anyone who told you that a relationship was 50/50 lied to you. Good relationships are 100/100. Each person has to give everything they can. That doesn't mean all the time, sometimes one person has to back away and the other person has to take over and that's ok. Do you really think Hammer is giving as much to those babies as I am?

"He can't and that's ok, he's making up for it in other ways by taking care of me while I take care of those babies. That's the way a relationship really works. You can't give the same financially that Seether can and that's ok. That doesn't mean you won't ever help financially, it just means that right now your contribution is different than his."

"He put me on his account." I mumbled wiping the tears off my cheeks.

"Awesome, you're buying lunch then." Kat teased. "Listen, Seether has always been very generous with his money, he's always been really smart with it and he makes it hand over fist. Is financial security not a great way for him to take care of you?"

"Yeah, I guess so. I just don't want to be a burden to him, financially or otherwise."

"Then get a job." She said flippantly. "Don't be a burden but don't take the joy of taking care of you away from him."

"Where am I going to get a job?"

"I don't know, I'm sure you'll think of something. Did you ask Seether how he made his first million?" I shook my head no. "He built a computer program or something and sold it. Why can't you do that?"

"Huh," I said, suddenly thinking that I was being silly. Kat patted my knee then stood and left the room. It wasn't long before there was another knock and Aiden walked in and closed the door, leaning against it.

"I freaked you out." He said not moving closer.

"No," I said, shaking my head. "You didn't freak me out, I just ... I don't want to be a burden on you. You've already done so much for me I didn't want you to resent me one day 'cause you have more to give than I do."

"For someone so smart you sure are stupid some times." He chuckled and walked over to kneel in front of me. I scowled at him, completely insulted and about ready to lose my shit on him. "Stop it, stop thinking just listen. I love you; did you think that meant I loved only as long as you could pay your way? Or that one day I would want something back? The only thing I want from you is for you to love me." He said reaching up and gripping the sides of my neck and shaking me gently. "Do you love me?"

"Yes I love you but I don't need you to buy me a house." I said my tears falling anew.

"I know that, my buying a house isn't just for you. I want you to love the house but I'm buying it for me, too and for our future kids and our family. I was being completely selfish when I bought that house."

"You are not." I laughed and sniffed. "There's nothing selfish about you."

"There is so!" He exclaimed, acting insulted.

"Name one thing about yourself that is selfish, one time that you took something for yourself when you should have or could have given it to someone else."

"When I accepted your love and your body when I should have let someone more worthy of your beauty have you." He said seriously. "That's what I did that was so damn selfish and I'm going to continue to be selfish because I am never letting you go. You are mine forever."

I couldn't think of a damn thing to say and after that proclamation the only thing I could do was throw myself at him and wrap my arms around him.

"I'm sorry." I whispered finally.

"Don't be, I'll make sure you remember this every chance I get." I laughed at him and buried my head in his chest as he chuckled happily. "Get packing, we're moving in a week."

"What? A week? Why so soon?" I demanded.

"Because I want you to myself and I don't want to be quiet anymore. I want to hear you scream while I make you come and not worry about waking babies."

CHAPTER 17

Grace-Lynn

Two weeks later I was sitting on the floor in our living room unpacking Aiden's things. I didn't have anything so there was nothing for me to unpack. He already had his computers set up in the office and was in there working. I was about to get up and make another cup of coffee when there was a knock on the front door.

"Check the peephole!" Aiden called as I walked to the door.

"It's a glass door," I called back, "I can see right through it. It's Ashlyn." I opened the door and let my sister in, hugging her tightly. "Hey Sweetie."

"Wow, going for the minimalist look hey?" She said looking around the empty room. The only things in this room besides boxes were the built in shelves on either side of the fireplace.

"Yeah, you wanna go furniture shopping with me?" I said leading her back to the kitchen.

There at least was a table and chairs that I had found at the thrift store down the street. I had begged the girl at the store to hold onto it for me while I ran home and grabbed Aiden to go back with his truck to pick it up.

None of the six chairs were the same but they had all been refinished in a bright teal colour and matched the base of the table. The table top was finished in a dark mahogany colour and I had fallen in love with it as soon as I'd seen it.

"Aiden refuses to go with me, says we should do it all online but I can't. I've gotta sit on stuff before I buy it."

"Sure," She said laughing as I handed her a cup of her favourite hot chocolate. "You want to go now? I'm free for the rest of the day, I'll even drive."

"Are you sure?" I asked, knowing Ashlyn probably had some studying to do and she was avoiding it. She nodded and I decided I wasn't being a good sister if I didn't help her procrastinate. "I'll just tell Aiden we're going and go change, I'll be right back."

"I'll tell Aiden, you change." She said and walked towards the office. I shrugged and ran upstairs to the only room that actually had furniture besides the office.

Seether

"Aiden?" I turned to find Ashlyn at the door of the office looking very nervous.

"What's up?"

"Um, Grace-Lynn and I are going to shop for some furniture, but I wanted to ask you something first." She said twisting the hem of her shirt.

"Sure, anything."

"Um, there's a guy at school who's been bugging me . . ."

"What kind of bugging?" I asked, my senses suddenly hyper aware.

"Mostly name calling, but it started when I said I wouldn't go

113

out with him and now it's gotten worse. I came here after washing my car because he'd thrown an entire carton of eggs at it."

"What's his name, I'll deal with it." She gave me his name and smiled much more relaxed just as Pixie came into the room.

"Everything ok?" She asked looking from me to her sister. I nodded and winked at her, letting her know I'd tell her later.

"Just great!" Ashlyn exclaimed and tugged on Pixie's hand. "Let's go, I'm excited for this."

"Ok, anything you are adamant about us not getting?" Pixie asked me, referring to the furniture.

"Nope, you got your bank card?" I asked referring to the one attached to my account.

"Yes Aiden." She said and kissed me then left.

I quickly turned back to my computer and looked up the kid Ashlyn had told me about, then I called Axle, Hammer and Lo and asked them to meet me at the kids house on their bikes and to be as loud as possible.

When we had all arrived the neighbours were all out on their door steps watching, alerted by the loud bikes. The four of us waved to them as we walked up to the door of the kids house. When he answered he slowly looked up at me and smirked.

"What do you want?" He demanded crossing his arms over his chest.

"You know Ashlyn Cameron?"

"Yeah, so, what does that little tease want?" I didn't move but Hammer did. His fist flew so fast the kid didn't see it coming and Hammer had come by his name honestly.

"That little tease is my girlfriend's little sister." I said to the kid as he lay in his front entrance bleeding. "Stay the fuck away from her or a broken nose will be the least of your problems." We turned and walked away, seeing quite a few of the neighbours nodding and smiling and one was even clapping. We climbed on our bikes and rode away.

We decided it had been too long since we had gone out for a beer and just hung out so we ended up at a local sports bar watching a hockey game on the big screen tv.

"So seriously, what was that about?" Lo asked, taking a pull from his beer.

"That little shit has been harassing Pixie's sister at school, egged her car today. She asked me for help today." I explained shrugging.

"Fucker," Axle said, shaking his head.

"Glad I hit him," Hammer said, flexing his hand. "Kid's got a hard fucking head." We all chuckled at Hammer's mulish tone then turned back to the game.

By the time I got back to the house an hour later a moving truck was there and three big guys were carrying a large sofa in through the front door. I stood off to the side with my arms crossed over my chest and waited until they were through so I could go into my own house.

"Pixie!" I called when I finally got inside.

"Yeah?" she asked, coming from the kitchen.

"You buy the store?"

"Nope, just a living room set." She said proudly watching the men set up the reclining sofa against the wall opposite the fireplace.

It was dark grey leather and opposite it were two recliners, both a deep burgundy colour still wrapped in plastic. There was also a rug on the floor and three end tables and boxes in another corner with lamps inside.

"The TV is being delivered later."

"A big one?" I asked, eyeing her skeptically.

"Um, is sixty inches big?" she asked cheekily.

"Woman, marry me!" I joked and grabbed her around the waist.

Later that evening as we sat on our new furniture and watched a movie on our new TV I pushed pause and turned her to look at me.

"I was serious you know."

"About what?" she chuckled smiling up at me.

"About marrying me."

"What?" She snorted.

"Ok, so I was joking this afternoon but I was also serious, I want you to marry me."

"Aiden you're crazy, we've known each other three months, we can't get married."

"Why not? How long do you think Lo and Alana have known each other? Ten months and they're getting married this summer. And Axle and Brooke? Eight months, Hammer and Kat? Also ten months."

"Aiden, we're not them and we've had other stuff between us." She said trying to move away from me.

"I know and I'm not saying we should jump into getting married or anything like that. I'm only saying that I love you and I don't need to know you for a life time to know I want to marry you."

"Ok Aiden, I get it. I love you, too and I want to spend the rest of my life with you but let's not rush anything."

"All right." I agreed, turning the movie back on. Later after we had gone to bed I lay awake thinking about our conversation. I knew she was being honest with me and she did love me and she did want to marry me one day, I just had to remind myself not to rush her.

The next evening we sat at our kitchen table eating Chinese takeout. We had been apart the entire day while I worked in the office here and she had gone over to Kat's to help with the baby. I watched her eat her honey garlic pork and wondered what had changed.

"What?" She asked looking up at me.

"Are we different?"

"What do you mean?"

"Something has changed, I just don't know what."

"Since when?" she asked, putting her fork down.

"I don't know." I said shrugging and slumping back in my chair.

"Ok, let's go back to when we first met. I was a shivering, quivering traumatized mess and you were an over tired traumatized mess. I'd say you're no longer so over tired and neither of us are so traumatized as before. I'm not shivering or quivering anymore and I do feel more confident. Is it so bad if things change?"

"No," I said smiling, "Not bad at all. I just got so caught up in everything happening I didn't see it all actually happen."

She shrugged and smiled, "Sometimes that's the best way."

"Are you happy?"

"With you or in general?"

"Both."

"Yes, I am very happy with you and in general . . . I'm getting

117

there. I still feel like I'm missing a purpose but I don't know what my purpose is yet." She said shrugging.

"You mean like a job?"

"Yes and no. I don't know if I want a job so much as a career or a vocation. Something that I can feel like I'm making a difference doing."

"You mean like helping women in your situation?"

"Hmm, nice euphemism." She said smiling. I shrugged not wanting to discuss her rape and the man who perpetrated it. "No, I'm not there yet."

"What do you mean?"

Now she shrugged. "I don't feel like I'm ready for that. I'm still stuck in my own survival and that's ok, it's good and one day maybe I'll turn my experience into something positive for someone else. For right now though I need to live for me."

"So, what is your purpose going to be?"

"You?"

"I'm your purpose?"

"No, but yes, part of my purpose right now is just to love you and let you love me. But I know there's more and I need to figure out what that is."

"Have you thought about going to those group sessions Alana and Brooke mentioned before?"

"Yeah, there's one tomorrow night. I was thinking of going."

"You should. Maybe someone there can help you find your purpose." She nodded and we finished eating then cuddled up on the couch to watch another movie. We were settling into a routine and I was feeling very satisfied with it.

CHAPTER 18

Grace-Lynn

I was sitting in a coffee shop a week later with my sister laughing at her story of the boy who had been bothering her at school. I didn't know that the day we had gone furniture shopping she had asked Aiden for help, he hadn't mentioned it to me.

But now as Ashlyn told me about this boy with his broken nose and sullen expression I couldn't help but laugh and silently thank Aiden. All too soon Ashlyn grew serious again though.

"What was foster care like?" She asked timidly. I stared at her for a moment, knowing that she was worried I was going to tell her my life was horrible growing up and sure she felt guilty for her own easy life.

"It wasn't all bad." I replied finally. "I don't have any horror stories like some people. I was lucky and was mostly placed with people who cared about what they were doing and were foster parents because they wanted to help kids. There were a few who only took kids in for the paycheck, but for the most part I had a decent home, a bed and clean clothes and lots of food."

"And love? Did any of those people love you like parents should?"

I shrugged thinking back to some of the better homes I was in.

"No, not really but I can't blame them. I wasn't theirs and they were doing the best they could. It was more like living with lots of distant aunts and uncles."

"I'm sorry. When dad told me about you I begged him to find you and bring you home but he was always three steps behind your trail." I could see she was starting to tear up and I reached across the table and took her hand.

"It's ok Ashlyn, I know you tried and I came to terms with my life years ago. I'm ok."

"Yeah but if you hadn't been in foster care you might not have gotten involved with that gang and you wouldn't have been anywhere near D–"

"And I wouldn't have met Aiden or Kat or Brooke or anyone else over at the MC. I wouldn't give them up for anything. Say I wasn't in foster care but was adopted by another family but it was a bad situation. I might not have found you and I wouldn't have all the great things I do now. I'm not happy that D raped me, but I am resigned to the fact that it did happen and I am moving on with the good that came of it."

She sniffed and looked at me then nodded and whispered, "Ok."

We finished our coffee and started to walk back to mine and Aiden's house. It was nearing the end of March which meant that spring was almost in full bloom.

There hadn't been more than a skiff of snow all winter and now the tulips were starting to poke their heads out of the ground. It was warm out so we decided to walk to the coffee shop and leave Ashlyn's car at the house.

When we got to her car Ashlyn hugged me goodbye and drove away smiling again. I let myself into the house and went to find Aiden. He was of course in the office in front of all his computers typing furiously at something. I tried to sneak up on him but he always knew when I was near.

Sliding my hands down over his chest I nipped and sucked his ear lobe, dragging his t-shirt up his abs and chest.

"What are you up to?" He asked, chuckling.

"Hopefully I'm up to seducing you." I turned his chair and climbed onto his lap, kissing him deeply.

God I loved kissing Aiden, his lips were so soft and he tasted like heaven. He pushed my shirt up over my head and tossed it to the floor then pulled the sports bra I had chosen that morning off and tossed it after my shirt. I yanked his shirt off of him and dropped it beside us as he stood and lowered us to the floor.

When my back touched the floor I tensed slightly but didn't stop Aiden as he pulled my pants off my legs. But then he was over me, looming and my vision darkened and he was gone and D was there. I could feel the pain from the beating and it was dark in the room and I could hear D's harsh breathing and smell the stale cigarettes on his breath.

"No!" I screamed and pushed at the chest that was over me.

I shook my head and screamed again, kicking out and connecting with something hard. I flailed, swinging my arms until I was free and running from the room.

I ran straight for the bathroom in the master bedroom and turned the water on as hot as I could stand it then got in and sunk to the floor, sobbing.

Seether

Holy fuck, what the hell just happened? One minute, no not even a minute it was more like seconds, mere seconds between us laughing and loving and her freaking the fuck out. I don't know what I did to bring back the memory but I did. We had made love so many times since the first time at the condo after the explosion and not once had she freaked out.

Pixie had tensed a couple of times but it only took me saying her name to bring her back, or changing our position, but this time I didn't have time to do anything before she was screaming and kicking and then running from the room. I heard the shower in our room as I slowly followed her path up the stairs.

I sat on the edge of our bed with my head in my hands and waited for her to come out. I could hear her crying and I wanted so badly to go in and comfort her but I knew she wouldn't want that.

I knew she was still too traumatized for that, so I waited until the hot water must have run out and she had to get out of the shower. She opened the bathroom door and stood staring at me, holding her towel tight to her chest.

"I'm sorry." We both said at the same time. I shook my head at her and sighed, "You have nothing to apologize for, if you can tell me what it was that set it off I won't do it again."

She shook her head but didn't move from the bathroom, "I don't know specifically what it was."

"Do you want me to leave?" She frowned and looked down at the floor but then shook her head no. "How about I get you something to sleep in and you can have a nap?"

She looked up at me surprised then blinked and nodded, stepping just slightly into the room. I stood slowly so I wouldn't scare her more and walked over to the dresser. I pulled one of my t-shirts out of my drawer and held it out to her. She took it but couldn't put it on and hold the towel at the same time.

"Can I help you?"

She looked up again and bit her lip then nodded slightly. I took the shirt back and unfolded it and slid it over her head then helped her slip her arms into the sleeves as she let the towel drop to the floor.

"Climb into bed." I said and picked up the towel and hung it in the bathroom. When I turned around again she was huddled under the covers on my pillow. I smiled a little and sat again on the edge of the bed. "Do you want to watch a movie?"

"No," she whispered, "Will you lay down with me? Can I cuddle against your back?"

"Of course," I said knowing she always drew comfort from that. I waved her over a little as I took off my pants but left my underwear on and crawled under the blankets with her. She waited as I got comfortable then snuggled against me.

"The floor," I heard her whisper and I held my breath. "It was the floor against my back that set me off and then you pulled my pants off and came up over me . . . he did that. And I know you aren't him and you didn't and wouldn't hurt me. I know it's irrational I just couldn't stop it. Suddenly the room was dark and you were gone and he was there and I could smell the cigarettes he smoked and I could feel the pain from being kicked."

I let out my breath on a sigh as I felt her tears soak my back. "I'm so sorry baby." I said and felt her shake her head then eventually she fell asleep, breathing deeply if not completely evenly.

It was hours later I was still lying with Pixie sleeping at my back when the doorbell peeled through the house. I quietly got up and pulled my pants up and hurried downstairs so Pixie wouldn't wake up.

I opened the door to find Kat and Hammer on the front step with the babies bundled into strollers. I smiled and shushed them and motioned for them to come in.

"What are you sleeping in the middle of the day?" Hammer laughed punching my shoulder. I shook my head as I took AJ out of her stroller.

"Pixie had a bad day." I said quietly lifting AJ up to my shoulder. "She's up in bed resting."

"I hope she's ok." Kat said, frowning.

"She will be," I said smiling then turned to Hammer. "Beer?"

"Yes please!" Kat exclaimed as she fell onto the couch. Both Hammer and I looked at her like she was nuts. "What? I'm allowed to have a beer if I want to! I'm twenty-eight years old, remember? And I pumped some milk before we came over."

"TMI," I said walking to the kitchen. "You could've stopped with you being twenty-eight."

AJ was still so small I held her to my chest with one hand as I bent and reached in the fridge and pulled out three bottles of beer. When I got back to the living room Pixie was there holding one of the boys.

I held up a bottle to her with a questioning look but she shook her head no. I smiled and sat in one of the arm chairs and rocked my namesake.

"So, we came over for a reason." Hammer said suddenly, he was holding the other baby boy and rocking gently in the other arm chair.

"You mean besides drinking my beer?" I asked, taking a drink.

"Aiden," Pixie admonished me quietly. I winked at her and smiled.

"We were hoping you guys would be the baby's God-parents." Kat said, her gaze shifting from me to Pixie and back again.

"Wait, what?" Pixie asked, finally looking up from the baby. "What about Axle and Brooke?"

"Well . . . ok, here's our thinking and don't get mad." Kat said, sighing heavily. "We've thought about this a lot and let me tell you this was not an easy decision. Axle is fifteen years older than me, he's already in his forties, not that that's old, but he's not exactly twenty-six like Seether is. And he's starting his own family and busy as all hell. We thought about Lo and Alana but they already have six kids and if anything happened to us they would be taking on at least three more."

"What Kat is trying to say through all the babbling is that we really feel that you guys are the best option for our kids if anything were to happen to us." Hammer said his gaze drifting from Kat to Pixie and then to me.

"But don't feel obligated to say yes." Kat said quickly.

"Um . . ." Pixie said looking over at me. I shrugged and smiled at her. "You know we're probably going to start a family of our own as well right?"

"Oh of course, we never thought otherwise, but . . . ok, don't worry we're not upset or anything." Kat said, sitting back on the couch looking like she was about to cry.

"Oh shit," Pixie said, her eyes getting big. She jumped up and placed the baby she was holding in my arms with his sister and rushed over to Kat and pulled her friend into her arms. "I didn't say no! I'm saying yes! Right Aiden? We're saying yes, tell her!" Hammer and I smiled at each other and he tapped his beer bottle against mine.

"Yes Kat, we would be happy to take your children if anything, heaven forbid, were to happen to you and Hammer." I said chuckling as we watched the two sobbing women on the couch.

"Oh thank God!" Kat cried then laughed when Pixie said she needed that beer now. We ordered pizza for supper then Hammer and Kat took their babies home before it got too late and cold for them. Pixie and I cleaned up the living room and kitchen and then we were up in the bed room on either side of the bed staring at each other.

"We're not doing anything tonight but sleeping." I said to her, trying to put her at ease. She was still wearing the shirt I'd given her earlier but had taken off the sweat pants she had put on when she'd gone downstairs.

"Ok," She whispered and nodded, pulling back the covers on the bed. "Um, I'm not really tired though since I slept all afternoon, could we watch a movie? Or I could go back downstairs and watch a movie there if you want to sleep?"

"No, we'll watch a movie here, together." I said grabbing the remote off the stand by the bed and handing it to her. "Whatever you want."

She took the remote and scrolled through Netflix until she found something she liked and settled against the pillows as I climbed in beside her. She scooted over until she was cuddled up against me and I wrapped my arm around her shoulder.

As we settled into to watch the movie though she couldn't sit still, finally she pulled away from me and sat on her knees looking at me. I watched her quietly, waiting for her to tell me what she was doing or thinking and then she whipped her t-shirt off over her head.

She sat in front of me completely naked and as my gaze skimmed down over her beautiful skin my cock hardened but I didn't move towards her. This was about her, I knew that and I had to let her take the lead.

After a minute of letting me stare at her she shifted so she was straddling my hips and started grinding herself against me. I could feel she was wet through my boxers but still barely moved as she leaned forward and kissed me deeply. Her soft breasts brushed against my chest, making me crazy.

It wasn't until she whispered 'touch me' into my mouth that I finally lifted my hands to her thighs and gently ran my fingertips up to her back, holding her to me as I devoured her mouth.

When she pulled away to take a breath I leaned forward and sucked on her collarbone, then nipped it and lifted one of her breasts into my mouth and sucked hard on her nipple. She reached between us and moved my boxers then impaled herself on me and we both cried out as I sunk deep inside her.

"Fuck baby, my Pixie, I fucking love you." I whispered in her ear as she started a quick pace that quickly brought her to climax. I twisted so she was lying across the bed and I was over her. "Is this ok?"

She nodded and arched her hips up into mine and arched her neck, pushing her head back into the bed and closing her eyes. I drove into her, pushing her higher up the bed with each thrust.

Her mouth fell open and she moaned as I cupped her breast and sucked again on her nipple. She lifted her knees and wrapped her legs around my hips and clenched her inner muscles, milking my cock then cried out as I thrust into her one more time and came hard inside her.

I panted over her, my face buried in her throat.

"So um, I just had a thought . . ." She said, clearing her throat. "Remember how the first time we did this I said let's not use a condom because I had just finished my period and couldn't get pregnant?"

"Yeah?" I dragged the word out thinking I knew where she was going with this.

"Well, that was like, more than a month ago and we haven't used a condom once." I reared up and looked down at her.

"Are you pregnant?"

"I don't know."

"Are you late?"

"Well, there's been so much going on I haven't really thought about it but I've got to be late, right? Like unless I get my period tomorrow. I mean, we haven't gone more than two days without having sex and don't women ovulate for like three days or something?"

"I don't know the secret inner workings of a woman's body Pixie." I said shaking my head.

"I didn't do it on purpose." She said quickly.

"What? I know that, I was there, too. I could have put a condom on at any time." I said chuckling at her as I rolled over to lie beside her. "If you are pregnant are you ok with that?"

"Well, I kind of don't have a choice do I?"

"Well yeah, you don't have to be happy about it, but I would hope that you wouldn't consider abortion an option." I said leaning up on my elbow to look down at her.

"Oh, Aiden no, never," She said adamantly, shaking her head.

"Well then if you don't get your period tomorrow then we'll go and get a test. Then we'll know one way or another and we can . . . I don't know, figure shit out I guess."

"You don't think this is bad?"

"No, why would this be bad?" I scowled down at her. "You love me right? And I love you, all good."

"Yeah," She chuckled, "But I was just raped three months ago, isn't it weird that now I'm super happy and possibly about to have a baby?"

"Nah," I said falling back onto my pillow then levering up again to situate us under the blankets and turn the forgotten movie off. "Everyone heals in their own way in their own time. Who's to say this isn't the right way for you?"

"Huh," she said, staring up at the ceiling.

"Go to sleep," I said and kissed her cheek, wrapping an arm over her waist and cuddling in next to her. I knew though that she stayed up for hours thinking about it.

CHAPTER 19

Seether

The next morning before Pixie got out of bed I ran to the closest drug store and picked up no less than five pregnancy tests. When I got home she was in the kitchen drinking a coffee.

"Period?" I asked, watching her closely.

She smirked at me then shook her head, "No but that doesn't mean it won't come later." I grunted at her and handed her the bag. "Aiden there are five tests in here."

"Six, one of the boxes has two tests in it. Go do one, quick." I ordered and pushed her out of the kitchen.

"Good grief." She huffed but went into the half bath we had on the main floor of the house. She came out a few minutes later and resumed her position, leaning against the kitchen counter and drinking her coffee.

"Well?" I demanded not understanding why she was so calm.

"I don't know." She said, shrugging. "The instructions said it took a few minutes."

"Are you freaking out?"

"No, I did a lot of thinking last night with you snoring in my ear."

"I don't snore." I pointed at her.

She giggled then continued, "I did think a lot about it last night. If I am pregnant then I am and I will be happy about it because it will be our baby and if I'm not then that's ok because it's not meant to be yet. Kat said it last night, we're both still young, hell I'm not even twenty-two yet."

"You might not be twenty-two yet but that was the most fucking mature thing I've ever heard." I said staring at her with my hand on my hips. "Now go look at that damn test." She snorted and giggled again then rushed to the bathroom. When she didn't come back right away I followed her and found her staring at the test in her hand, a disappointed look on her face.

"I'm sorry baby." I said pulling her into my arms.

"It's ok," She said hugging me back. "It's just not meant to be yet right?"

"You know you never saw a doctor after you were raped, maybe you should make an appointment and get checked out. Just to make sure you're ok." I said, pulling back from her slightly. "D beat you up pretty bad, who knows what he could've done inside, and it can't hurt right?"

"Yeah I guess." Pixie said then looked up at me. "Will you go with me?"

"Of course."

Grace-Lynn

And that's how we ended up sitting in a waiting room at a doctor's office surrounded by pregnant women. As we sat and waited more women came and went in varying stages of pregnancy and I couldn't help but feel a little jealous. Especially when a woman who was obviously about to blow sat beside us.

"How far along are you?" She asked, smiling widely. "Can't be far, you're not even showing."

"Oh, no we're not pregnant." I said smiling back at her. "We're here for other reasons." I said nodding then turning to Aiden pleading with my eyes for him to get this woman to stop talking to me.

Just then my name was called by the nurse and I was saved. I hustled after the nurse as Aiden followed me chuckling quietly.

"Not funny." I said when the nurse had left us in the exam room.

We sat for a few minutes in silence before the doctor knocked and entered the room.

"Hello, I'm Doctor Smith, it says here you're not here for a prenatal visit? What can I do for you?"

"Hi Doctor," I said, shaking her hand. "Um we know you're busy so we won't keep you. I was raped just over three months ago and beaten pretty badly."

"I'm so sorry to hear that." The doctor said sympathetically.

"Uh, thank you, um I've had a lot of help with my recovery." I chuckled looking at Aiden. "Um, my boyfriend and I have been having sex for over a month without condoms and we haven't gotten pregnant. We realized that I was never really checked out after the attack and we were just wanting to make sure that nothing the man attacked me did hindered my ability to get pregnant."

"Oh," the doctor said somewhat surprised. "Ok, how about you lie back and pull your shirt up a little bit?" I did as I was asked and the doctor palpated my stomach gently. "Does that hurt at all?"

"No," I said, shaking my head.

"Is there still vaginal trauma that you know about?" she asked, putting my shirt back.

"I don't think so," I said, shrugging looking at Aiden who shrugged back at me. "Um, I have no pain at all when we have sex."

"That's good, and you orgasm? You have regular fluid secretion?"

"I think so, it seems to be normal anyway."

"And there's no blood in your urine or anything like that?"

"Nope."

"Were you sodomized?" I looked at her shocked and she shook her head apologetically. "I'm sorry, you've been so straightforward and honest with your answers to this point, I should have been more sensitive to your situation."

"No it's ok, it just took me off guard, no one asked that before but no, I wasn't."

"Ok, that's good. Have you had a period since you were raped?"

"Yes, it was right before we had sex the first time, almost two months ago, the first week of February?"

"And you took a home test?"

"Yes it was negative."

"Ok, well that could have been a false negative but given the amount of trauma you experienced I would like for you to have an ultrasound done to check for any damage to your uterus or fallopian tubes. I don't think there's anything to be concerned about but it's always good to check these things out. Before the rape, did you have regular periods and cycles?"

"I think so, I'm only twenty-one so I figured that one period a month was pretty regular even if they weren't always twenty-eight days apart."

"Ok, well I will send the requisition for the ultrasound and the lab will call you when they have an opening then you can call the nurses up front here for an appointment a week after that. Are you trying to get pregnant? Or was this an oops that got you thinking?"

"Definitely the second one," I chuckled "and we have no plans to start trying now we just want to be careful."

"Ok, no worries, we'll get this all straightened out." As we left the doctor's office I felt a lot better about things, no we didn't have any more answers now than when we walked into the office but things were rolling forwards.

When we got home Brooke and Axle were standing at our front door kissing with Imogen in the stroller beside them.

"Seriously?" Aiden demanded "Go home and make out!" They laughed at him as he let us all in the door. I quickly took Imogen out of her stroller and snuggled her up in my arms and took a deep breath.

"Mm, she still has the new baby smell." I said smiling.

"It's baby shampoo." Axle said irritably and tried to take his daughter from me.

"Don't even!" I exclaimed, moving away from him, "I've had a bad day and I need me some baby cuddles."

"What?" Brooke demanded pushing past Axle, "What kind of bad day, David, leave the girl alone."

"Nothing really bad, we just thought maybe we could be pregnant but we're not." I said shrugging.

"Oh sweetie, I'm sorry." Brooke said sympathetically.

"It's ok. We're really not trying it just came to me all of a sudden last night that I haven't had a period –"

134

"Stop!" Axle demanded and rushed out of the living room to the kitchen then called back, "Ok, you can keep going, I can't hear you anymore, Seether get your ass in here and distract me from your woman's loose tongue!" Aiden snorted and followed Axle into the kitchen.

"What are you doing?" We heard Aiden demand, "It's not even noon and you're having a beer?"

"After that shit your woman just spouted I need it! Hell I deserve it for surviving that shit!"

Brooke and I chuckled then settled on the couch to talk. "So," She said, reminding me "You haven't had a period . . ."

"Yeah, since the beginning of February and we haven't been using condoms so I thought maybe but no. Well, probably not anyway. I did a home test this morning and it showed up negative but the doctor said it could have been a false negative and scheduled me for an ultrasound. We were just worried that D had broken something." I shrugged, "I guess we'll have to wait and see."

Just then Aiden came back into the room with two cups of steaming tea, set them on the side tables on either end of the couch and left again. I watched him go with so much love and I knew that it didn't matter if we ever had babies, he was all I needed.

"Well, I know that look," Brooke said smiling.

"Yeah," I sighed like a love sick fool, "I kinda love him a lot."

"Well the whole reason we came here in the first place besides a walk in the nice weather was to invite you to Imogen's baptism on Sunday." Brooke said smiling sweetly at her baby, sucking like the devil on her soother.

"Oh we'd love to be there!" I exclaimed happily. "At the Cathedral?"

"Yeah, after the eleven am mass though not during."

"Are Lo and Alana Imogen's God-parents?"

"Yeah, pretty obvious?"

"Well, if I had to guess," I laughed. "Lo and Axle have been friends since childhood and they started the MC together. You and Alana were friends before the guys and technically didn't she introduce you to Axle?"

"Yeah, no technically about it," Brooke laughed. "She totally introduced me to David."

"We would love to be at your baby's baptism." I said laughing.

CHAPTER 20

Seether

Sunday dawned bright and early with Pixie curled up in pain.

"Cramps," She moaned from the shower. "Fucking period."

Well hell, I guess we knew for sure now that she wasn't pregnant.

"Are you gonna be ok babe?" I asked standing outside the shower.

"Yeah, I just wish this had come yesterday, or tomorrow. The first day is always the worst and I don't have time to curl up in a ball today." She said moaning again.

"Anything I can to help?"

"Advil, lots of Advil and if you could find a way for me to walk around with a heating pad all day that would be good too." She sighed then cursed her body again.

I wasn't sure how I was going to get a heating pad for her at the church, a hot water bottle wouldn't stay hot enough and I knew she wasn't going to miss Imogen's baptism for anything.

"I think we're out of Advil, I'm going to run to the drug store and get some more." I called to her over the water and ran out of the house before she could remind me of the bottle above the fridge.

I ran to the drug store and walked up and down the feminine hygiene aisle with absolutely no clue what I was looking for. Finally the pharmacist seemed to take pity on me and asked if I needed any help. I almost fell at her feet and kissed the ground she walked on.

I explained the situation to her and she nodded then took me over and grabbed a couple of bottles of pain killers just for PMS symptoms. I actually hugged her and as I rushed down the first aid aisle to the till I noticed those pain wraps that heated up and there was a box that said menstrual.

"Would this be a bad idea?" I asked the pharmacist.

"I don't see why," She replied shrugging. "If your girlfriend said heat helped and she's not pregnant and has no other medical conditions it can't hurt." I nodded and grabbed two boxes, paid for my items then rushed home. I ran into our room just as Pixie was pulling black leggings up her legs.

"You know we have Advil here right?" She said smirking at me, not quite standing up right.

"I know, but I figured there had to be something else that would help. You said you wanted heat but I can't imagine you could take an actual heating pad to the church with you but what about this?" I pulled one of the boxes out of the bag and handed it to her.

"Huh," She said as she stared at it.

"The pharmacist said as long as you weren't pregnant and didn't have any medical conditions listed on the box it should be ok." I hurried to explain.

"Huh," She murmured again. She pulled one of the pads out of the box and fitted it against her stomach just under the waistband of her underwear and waited. It didn't take long before it began to heat up and Pixie began to relax with the heat. "Oh my God that is so amazing! Why have I never seen these before?"

"I don't know, I think they were in a stupid place considering. I mean I know the brand is for muscle aches and pains but really if it's for menstrual cramps it should be with other menstrual products right?"

She laughed at me and straightened up to stand normally. "Yeah, I agree but now that you've found them we're going to have to buy stock in the company."

"Done," I said and planned to do that first thing in the morning, making a note to call Jeff Edwards at the bank. "Now, finish getting dressed, we've gotta get over to the church."

Even though neither of us were Catholic we went to mass with Brooke, Axle, Lo, Alana and her family. Kat and Hammer were also there but sat at the back so they could escape quickly if one of the babies made a fuss.

When mass was over and the church mostly empty we all gathered at the front and watched the priest baptize Imogen. She mostly slept through the whole thing until the priest poured the water over her head, then she wailed like the hounds of hell were after her.

Bad comparison? Axle thought so.

We were leaving the church to head over to the newly renovated clubhouse for a celebratory lunch when we were halted by the sound of a gunshot. The street was mostly empty that time of day on a Sunday and as we all crouched in the front steps of the church all we heard was halting footsteps coming towards us.

"You fuckers have messed with me for the last fucking time." We all looked over to see Little D standing at the bottom of the steps pointing a gun at us. "You're all fucking dead."

"D wait," Pixie said, stepping towards him holding her hands out in front of her.

"Pix –"

"No," She said looking over to me and shaking her head slightly. She was trying to tell me something without saying it. I didn't get it until I looked at her hands. One was folded in the ASL sign for 'I love you' then she turned away from me again and moved towards Little D.

"D, I've been waiting for you to come and get me." She said, taking a step towards the man with the gun. When I looked closer at him I saw that his leg was bleeding and even from this far away there was a horrible odor coming from him.

"What the fuck are you talking about?" D's voice was laced with pain and I knew something wasn't right with the man.

Grace-Lynn

"D, I thought you were coming to get me." I said taking another step towards D. He was limping and his grip on the gun was unsteady, his eyes were feverish and he was sweating. It was warm out but not that warm. "Why did you take so long to come get me, D?"

"Gracie you're fucking crazy," D slurred confused by my words but letting me get closer to him step by step. "I was never coming to get you. I came here to kill all of you."

"You can't kill me D, you love me, you said so." I replied softly. I was almost to the bottom step in front of him and before I could say anything else Aiden was flying past me, punching D in the face and knocking him out then kicked D's gun away from him.

"Fuck, what is that smell?" he demanded covering his nose and gagging then he turned to me and got right in my face. "Don't you ever fucking do that again you hear me? You don't tell me you love me and then put yourself in danger like that! Someone call 911 before I fucking kill this son of a bitch." Aiden muttered, pulling me against his chest and rocking me back and forth.

Later as we all sat around the fire pit behind the clubhouse we talked about what could have happened today. D had us all cornered in that stairwell and if he'd opened fire we all would have died.

"We had some angels looking out for us today." Brooke said quietly, snuggling into Axle with Imogen in her arms.

"Well, no more sadness," Alana said after a few minutes. "It's time to be happy. D is gone, Briggs is gone, Michaels is gone. We are a family here together. Lo and I finally set a date for our wedding."

"It's about damn time." Axle muttered, squeezing Brooke and kissing her temple.

"No shit," Hammer said, rocking one of the boys in his car seat. Aiden chuckled from our side of the fire with AJ in his arms and Kat was curled up with the other baby boy beside Hammer.

"Well, as soon as school is out this summer, you've got a week and then we're getting married at the Cathedral." Lo snorted at his friends.

"Even better than that, at Easter Lo is being baptized in the church." Alana said and we all watched as Lo blushed.

"Fuck, seriously man?" Axle asked a huge grin splitting his face. "That's fucking awesome, congratulations."

"You're next." Lo said to him pointing at his friend.

"Yeah, I think I am," Axle murmured into Brooke's hair.

Bonus: War Angels Wedding

Alana – 18
25 Years Ago

Walking through the mostly empty halls of the university I shifted my books in my arms before I dropped them all. I have to admit running into the wall was partially my fault.

"Crap!" I exclaimed as my books all tumbled from my arms to the floor. I heard multiple masculine voices laughing as I crouched to pick the books up.

"Shit, sorry," One distinct voice said and crouched in front of me and helped gather my books.

"Thanks," I mumbled as the guy helped me stand up. I looked up into the smiling, clean ocean blue eyes of Mike Martin, hottest guy in school, basketball team captain and all around golden boy. "Uh, thank you," I stuttered and stepped around him, heading towards the dorms.

I hurried down the hall to more masculine laughter and was almost out the door when Mike caught up to me.

"Wait, you're Alana right?" Mike asked, opening the door for me.

"Uh, yeah," I said stepping through the door.

"I'm Mike." He said walking with me.

I snorted looking up at him, "Everyone knows that." Mike's hair was still wet from the shower and he pushed it back sheepishly.

"Uh, the guys and I are going out for a beer, do you want to come with us?"

"Oh," I replied surprised, "Would I be the only girl?"

"I'm sure the guys'll have girls there but I doubt they'll be the kind you usually hang out with." He shrugged.

"Oh? And what kind of girls will be at the bar?"

"The easy kind," Mike shrugged again.

"Why are you asking me? I'm not the easy kind of girl."

"I know, I don't want the easy kind."

"What kind do you want?" I asked skeptically.

"The kind that will make me laugh, and challenge me, someone smarter than me."

"And you think that's me?"

"Yeah, I do."

"Oh," I said nodding, "I'll go for a beer with you." We dropped off my books in my dorm room then walked to Mike's truck talking about school and basketball.,

When we got to the bar, Mike's teammates were already at a table with girls draped all over them. Mike introduced me to his friends then left to get us a beer. One of the girls sidled up to me and nudged me with her boney hip.

"Lucky bitch," she smirked.

"What?"

"I hear his dick is huge. You're gonna have a good night."

"Uh . . . ok," The girl snorted and moved back to sit in the lap of one of the other guys. When Mike got back to the table one of his friends got his attention.

"There's a party across town, you in?"

"What do you think; you want to go to a party?" Mike asked me.

"Oh no, but you go ahead." I said shaking my head.

"We're out Clarke." Mike said and turned back to me.

"Fuck man, give the bitch back her ovaries and grow your balls back, let's go party."

"Shut the fuck up Clarke," Mike said over his shoulder.

"You wanna fuck the fat bitch do it and move the fuck on." Clarke yelled back. I could feel the heat creeping up my face and tears welling in my eyes as Mike's friends laughed at Clarke's comments. Before I knew what was happening Mike had whirled and punched Clarke so in the face he fell off his chair onto the floor.

"Grow the fuck up Clarke." Then Mike took my hand and pulled me out of the bar and back to his truck. When we got there he punched the door of his truck twice then turned to lean back against it, burying his face in his hands.

"Fuck," He muttered, shoving his hair back off his forehead. "I'm really sorry about Clarke, he's always been a massive douche."

"It's ok," I replied shrugging, "I know what I look like, just no one's ever said it like that before."

"What does that mean?" Mike demanded.

"Oh come on Mike, I know I'm overweight, I'm not model thin like those girls in there." I scoffed.

"Thank fuck!" Mike exclaimed, "You're fucking perfect the way you are."

"Well I like the way I look, it took me a long time to be comfortable in my own skin but I am."

"Good because I think you're beautiful. You're feminine and you're built the way a woman should be." We stared at each other for a while and eventually noise from the bar broke our trance.

"Come on, let's get you home and put ice on your hand." I said smiling and walking around the truck. "I'd hate for the coach to be mad because you can't play in the championship game next week because of me."

I did take Mike home that night and put ice on his hand. We talked more but nothing besides a really sweet goodnight kiss happened.

Over the next week we spent every waking moment together that we weren't in classes. I even went to his practices. The day of the championship game dawned early for him and I knew I wouldn't see him until the game that night.

I was nervous for him and I tried to make myself busy cleaning and studying and I even went to church but nothing really helped. My mother would say let go and let God but I was too young to really understand what that meant.

Finally fans were allowed into the gymnasium where the game was being played. None of my friends liked basketball and they all refused to go with me. One even said I shouldn't bother going either because Mike was probably just using me. I shrugged at her and shook my head.

Mike wasn't using me. He hadn't pressured me for anything more than a few kisses. He knew I didn't want a serious relationship until I graduated and he agreed we would be friends who studied together . . . and kissed and held hands.

So here I was watching the championship game with bated breath. There was only two minutes left on the clock and we were behind by one point. We needed either a three pointer or two baskets to win. Mike had possession of the ball and he was standing just outside the three point line yelling directions to the rest of the team.

At just one minutes left on the clock with the shot clock counting down one of the defenders charged. Mike twisted and dribbled out of the way and took a jump shot.

I don't know about him but for me time slowed until the world around us erupted. The ball swished through the net just as the buzzer went and three points were added to the scoreboard. We . . . no Mike won the game!

As all the fans swarmed the court to celebrate, Mike was raised up on his teammates shoulders. I stayed in the stands not wanting to get crushed. When Mike saw me standing there smiling like an idiot he made his friends put him down then he pushed and shoved through the crowd, climbing the stand to me.

Before I could say or do anything he had wrapped me in his arms and was kissing me deeply. When he finally pulled back I laughed.

"Mike you're all sweaty," He just laughed at me and kissed me again.

Lo – 19
25 Years Ago

I was sitting on the edge of the field watching the football team

I used to be a part of run drills while the coach yelled at them. It was a bright sunny day, if not super warm.

"I'm done," I looked over as my best friend David slumped on the ground beside me. A new bruise was blooming on his cheek and I knew he'd gotten into it with his step-dad again.

"You signed up?" I asked him. We had talked a long time about what to do after high school. Neither of us wanted to go to college or university and without it we know we had no prospects. We decided to join the Canadian Armed Forces.

"Yeah I'm in, gotta report tomorrow morning, you?"

"Same," I replied, "Either we're completely insane or this will be the best time of our lives."

"See the world and kill terrorists and get paid doing it. Hoo-ah!"

"That's the Marines," I laughed.

"It applies," David said, shoving my shoulder.

Alana – 23
20 Years Ago

"Mike stop hesitating, I'm ready." I kept telling him.

"I know, I just don't want to hurt you." He said for the hundredth time. Here we were, in the honeymoon suite of a nice hotel on our wedding night and he was hesitating.

"Mike sweetie, you've been making me hot and bothered for five years. Now we can finally make love, you are naked, I am naked, I am really hot and bothered, please kiss me and –"

And he did, he kissed me and all thought flew out of my brain and then I felt a pinch as he thrust inside me. He pulled away and kissed all over my face, not moving, letting me get used to his invasion. It didn't take long before the pain was gone and the sensations were completely different.

"Oh God Mike!" I cried as he started to move. It didn't take long and I'm pretty sure I didn't orgasm that night but it was still utterly spectacular.

We had both graduated for university a year before and had started dating for real while we got our careers started. We had bought a small house that we would start moving into in the morning. We had a plan, we were going to build our lives for a few years, save some money and then we would discuss children.

I was ok with this plan, but we were both also open to anything happening. If we became pregnant before then so be it and if not then so be it.

Life was good for Mike and I. We had five years of happiness, full of each other and job promotions. We were happy but we knew something was missing.

Lo – 25
18 Years Ago

"Come on Lieutenant, we've been invited by some locals to a gentlemen's club." Our superior officer, Major Dorne said. He was following a young East Timorese boy up the street.

I looked at David who now preferred to be called Axle, a nickname given to him years ago by our mechanics teacher in high school. He looked as dubious as I did about this situation but we followed anyway.

The boy led us through the maze of streets and finally into a filthy little hut with just a rug over the door and no windows. The stench in the room was overwhelming and only the fearful eyes of little kids staring up at us kept us from running out again.

"These are just kids, Major." Axle said disgustedly.

"What's your point Second Lieutenant?" The Major asked using Axle's full rank, seemingly to put him in his place.

"The point sir is that these are kids." Axle repeated.

"Right, and do you know what kids have? Nice tight little pussy holes that squeeze even the smallest cock tight." The Major laughed, grabbing his crotch, "And I ain't got a small cock!"

Just as the Major turned away to pick a girl a flash of movement caught my eye. Axle was still trying to convince the Major we needed to leave as I followed what I was sure I couldn't have really seen. Blonde hair in an Asian country, couldn't be right?

I smacked Axle on the arm to get his attention then walked across the room being careful not to step on any of the kids crammed into the tiny room. Once I got to the corner I found a little girl huddled under some rugs. Her face was filthy and her hair was ratted and covered in mud but it was definitely blonde hair and those were definitely blue eyes staring up at me.

"What the fuck?" Axle demanded looking over my shoulder.

"You don't belong here." I said to the girl. "What's your name?"

"Picked one after all eh Bishop?" Major Dorne called laughing from across the room. We ignored him and kept our attention on the girl.

"We won't hurt you." I said to her, holding my hand out to her. She shrunk away from me and her eyes widened in fear.

"How many times do you think she's heard that?" Axle asked angrily.

"How old are you?" The girl looked from me to Axle and back again.

"One time," She whispered hoarsely, "Not two."

"We don't want that." I said shaking my head. "We want to get you out of here and back to your family."

"No family." She said, tears starting to track down her cheeks.

"Hey!" A shout sounded from the side of the room. "You there, make choice and go, no talk!"

Axle turned and went to talk to the owner of this so-called gentlemen's club. I ignored them knowing Axle would do what was necessary to get this girl out of here.

"Come on," I said holding my hand out again. "Let's get you out of here."

Finally the girl took my hand and let me lead her out of the brothel. There was another shout from the owner as we left but Axle silenced him. We didn't get any more information from the girl as we walked and by the time we dropped her off at the base hospital we were called into the commander's office.

Walking in the office we were greeted by the Lieutenant Colonel and Major Dorne.

"Gentlemen," The LC said as we stood at attention in front of his desk. "At ease men." We relaxed slightly into parade rest position. "I understand you stole a prostitute from a brothel in town?"

"Yes sir," We both answered at the same time.

"What is your reason for this?"

"The girl couldn't be more than ten years old and she has blonde hair and blue eyes." I answered, looking straight ahead.

"What does that have to do with anything?" The LC demanded though I knew he had to know what that meant.

"It means sir that this girl does not belong in East Timor, how did she get here sir?" Axle asked and I could feel him getting angrier and angrier as Major Dorne stood in the corner smirking.

"Gentlemen what were you doing in this brothel to begin with?"

"We were led there by a superior officer sir. We were told it was a gentleman's club." I answered knowing this answer would either get us into a shit load of trouble or not.

"A gentleman's club?"

"Yes sir." We both answered.

"Who was the superior officer?"

"Major Dorne, sir." I answered.

"That's interesting Winters because Major Dorne here tells me you led him there. The Major says he was only there to keep you out of trouble."

"That is incorrect, sir." I said still not making eye contact with Major Dorne whose face was turning a bright red. "The Major told us we had been invited by some locals to go to a gentlemen's club. We then followed a young boy through the streets of the city to a hut. Inside the hut we found many young Asian children. While in the hut I caught a movement and found a young female child in the corner of the room. Second Lieutenant Bishop and I convinced the girl to come with us and we took her to the base hospital."

"Sir Winters is lying." Dorne said from the corner.

"I don't think so Major, Winters and Bishop have always been honest and have exemplary records where as you are known to visit local brothels and whore houses." The LC didn't take his eyes off of Axle and I as he spoke to Dorne. The girl will be taken care of and all efforts will be made to return her to her family. Dismissed, all of you."

Alana – 27
15 Years Ago

"Come on baby, push!"

"Mike, you push!" I muttered to him as I did indeed push. What the fuck was I thinking? Sure, let's have a baby! It'll be great! Sure, five months of all-the-damn-time sickness, getting fat, no coffee and now the worst pain imaginable. Yup, let's have a baby!

"I wish I could push for you baby but you're so close."

"Don't you say baby to me Mike." I said relaxing once the contraction subsided.

"Ok," The doctor said, "I can see the head, one more good push and the head will be out. On the next contraction, ready . . . go . . ."

So, I pushed and pushed and pushed and a few short minutes, although those minutes felt a lot longer, we had our baby boy. Nathanial George; family name, he was so sweet and for the next year we loved on him like no parents ever loved on a baby before. And then I completely lost my mind and said to Mike, "Let's have another baby."

Once we started trying to get pregnant there was no stopping us, after Nate we had Caleb Jeffery, then we decided to take a break from having kids. Just for a little while and that lasted two years and Jack Jordan came along. Not even two years after that Link William arrived in our world and for a long time our world was complete.

We had our boys, and they were busy. I had quit working after Link was born and started a day home. It was the easiest way I could think of to make money and stay home with my boys.

Our days were full of making lunches and getting the boys to school, then building projects and Lego houses and bases. Soon we were into dinosaurs and wrestling.

Just as Link was ready to go into Kindergarten I decided to close up my day home and go back to work. Mike was working full time managing an oil field company office. His degree had been in business management and he was certainly making it work for him and for us.

He had continued his learning and had taken many courses to make him more marketable in the oil field industry. Since the majority of jobs around where we lived had to do with drilling oil out of the ground it only made sense.

We became entrenched in our little community, we went to church, our boys went to the local Catholic school, Mike and I coached different summer sports teams from soccer to base-ball. We were a happy family, and then one day it all came crashing down.

Lo – 32
10 Years Ago

"Welcome to the war!" Axle hollered at me over the explosions of mortar fire. Our position had been compromised and here we sat like ducks waiting for the Taliban to move on. "Holy fuck am I ready to go home!"

"You and me both brother!" I called back to him then ducked again as gun fire erupted over our heads. "LC, what are your orders sir?"

"Stay put!" our superior officer hollered at us over the radio. "Do not engage unless absolutely necessary!"

"Fucking hell!" Axle spit, "Does he not realize this might be necessary?"

"We wait!" I yelled back to Axle. The rest of our assault squadron was just as pinned down though in a slightly safer area behind us on the mountain. After being involved in Operation K-bar back in 2001 we thought we had seen it all. This tour was only supposed to be IED clearing and tracking down what was left of the Taliban and al-Qaeda leaders.

"Next time we get the chance we're going to the Olympics! Whoever the fuck got assigned to Vancouver are a bunch of lucky sons of bitches!"

"Yeah that would've been nice." I agreed just as the shooting overhead stopped. We waited quietly for a few more minutes then slowly inched out of our hiding place. There were dead bodies scattered all over the road and burning and mangled trucks dotted the edges of it, the road that could barely be considered a goat trail up the mountain. "Next time we have the choice to re-up let's not. I think we've done our country proud."

"I think we've done most countries proud." Axle replied standing beside me and looking over the carnage left after a local tribe got in the way of a group of Taliban fighters. Men, women and children were left to rot in the sun.

"Call in some help and let's get these people buried." I mumbled and radioed back to our commander who was holed up with the rest of our squadron on the mountain. "Sir the fighting has stopped for now, me and Axle are going to start the cleanup."

"Negative Lieutenant, we do not have time to dig graves. We will radio back to base and have someone else take care of it," was the reply.

"Sir I don't believe we have time for that."

"Too bad, we need to keep moving. Those caves will not clear themselves."

"Fuck." Axle exclaimed angrily. Slowly we continued out of our hidey hole and continued up the road, weapons drawn and pointed ahead, each step a chance at not making it home. "Three more fucking years and I'm going home and staying there."

"I'm with ya brother, no more orders from commanders with commendations and medals on their minds while innocent people lay dying on the side of a dirt road."

"What are you going to do when we get home?"

"I don't know man." I answered pausing as a movement caught my attention from the corner of my eye. Axle, always in tune with me stopped as well and waited. We both crouched, making ourselves smaller targets as we looked closely at the surrounding terrain. There didn't seem to be anything around but dirt and rocks and death.

When nothing moved after five minutes and no one jumped out at us I decided I must have been mistaken about seeing something, either that or it was an animal running away. I stood again and started walking up the hill just as slowly as before.

"You gonna go home and cuddle up with Janine?"

"You mean Jeanette?" I said correcting Axle on the name of the girl I had been cuddled up with the last time we went home. "Nah, got a letter saying she found the love of her life and she was getting married."

"Shit, sorry man."

"No worries, I knew it wouldn't last." I said, shrugging slightly. "What about you? You gonna reconnect with your sister?"

"I don't know if her dad lets me maybe."

"How old is she now?"

"Eh, probably about sixteen or seventeen," Axle replied then stopped suddenly and dropped to the ground in a crouch. I followed him and looked around hoping to see or hear what he did. "There's something over there." He murmured, pointing his weapon at the brush to the south side of the road. Just then we heard an animal scurry through the brush and the entire world came crashing down.

The flash of a land mine set off by a desert snake sent us flying backwards and landing against the side of the mountain knocking Axle unconscious and breaking at least two of my ribs and possibly giving me a concussion.

"Fuck!" I exclaimed on a harsh breath as pain flooded my body. "Ax, wake up." I nudged him knowing that probably wasn't good for him if there was something seriously wrong with him but I had to wake him up.

It might have been a snake that set off the mine but the explosion would bring Taliban fighters down the mountain from the caves in minutes and we needed to get the fuck outta Dodge.

I took stock of my own injuries and decided I was going to have to go for it. I laid Axle flat on the ground and rolled over him pulling him up with my momentum into a fireman's carry.

The technique was called a Ranger Roll and it was very effective when trying to lift a very heavy man like Axle who was completely unconscious and wasn't going to be helping lift themselves up.

The Ranger Roll didn't help my ribs feel any better and as I stood getting my bearings under Axle my concussion was making me feel a little dizzy but I didn't have time to care. I had to get us back to our squadron and get us the fuck out of Afghanistan.

Just as I reached the spot where we had hidden before a patrol of fighters came walking out of the darkness behind us. I dropped a moaning Axle off my shoulders and followed him down to the ground and covered his mouth. His eyes flew open and I tried to convey to him how important it was for him to stay quiet. He nodded slightly and calmed his breathing.

We waited for about ten minutes before the entire patrol had passed by us and we could speak quietly if freely.

"Forgive me LT, but haven't we been in this particular fox hole before? It looks mighty familiar." Axle rasped looking around and breathing heavily.

"Fuck you," I muttered and rolled over onto my back. "That blast broke at least two of my ribs; you get to carry me the rest of the way down this fucking God forsaken mountain."

Alana – 35
7 Years Ago

"Nate, answer the door please!" I called from the kitchen. The doorbell had gone off twice and I was busy trying to drain spaghetti noodles and get supper on the table. Mike should be home any minute and whoever was at the door was really starting to piss me off. Better not be a sales person cause I might take whatever they're selling and shove it up their ass.

"Mom! It's the police!" Nate called back and I heard his feet run from the door and disappear into the house.

"What did you do?" I jokingly called after him and I walked to the front door. "Hello Constable, what can I do for you?"

"Ma'am," One of the officers said politely, "I'm Constable Anderson and this is Constable Weeks, could we come in for a moment?"

"Of course," I said stepping back from the door. "Was it my kids?"

"Ma'am?"

"I have four boys; I'm sure whatever the issue if they were involved it will be rectified."

"Oh, no ma'am your children aren't involved in anything that we know of." Constable Weeks replied shaking her head. "Ma'am, is your husband Michael Martin?"

"Uh, yeah, he should be home in a few minutes if you need to speak to him." I said confused. Why on earth would the police want to talk to Mike?

"Ma'am could we please sit?" Constable Anderson said motioning into the house.

"Uh, sure," I said leading the officers into the living room just off the front entrance. Just then the front door opened and my best friend, Christine rushed in.

"Alana, I saw the police car outside, is everything ok?" She demanded slamming the door behind her.

"I don't know, the Constables were just about to tell me." I replied as she came around the couch and sat beside me.

"What's this about?" Christine demanded, never one to beat around the bush.

"Mrs. Martin, your husband was in a car accident this morning." Constable Weeks said softly.

"What?" I demanded.

"No, Mike drives like an old lady, there's no way he was in a car accident." Christine said, chuckling nervously.

"I'm afraid his car hit a patch of ice and he lost control of the vehicle. The car slid across the center line and collided head on with a pickup truck. Your husband was killed instantly, I'm very sorry." Constable Anderson said as gently as he could.

"No, Mike will be home in just a few minutes." Christine said, shaking her head. I looked over at her and took her hand. I must be in shock, that's why I wasn't reacting and Christine seemed to be losing her mind.

"Um, what about the other driver...or passengers...were there any other casualties?" I asked, frowning. I looked over at Christine and saw the tears running down her cheeks. Why were my cheeks dry? Why wasn't I more upset?

"No ma'am there wasn't any other casualties or injuries," Constable Weeks said and she seemed to be getting farther and farther away. My vision blurred and suddenly Christine was calling my name but I couldn't seem to make myself answer her and then everything was gone.

We buried Mike two weeks later in a very small service with just our families and closest friends present. I had found out the morning he died that I was pregnant with our fifth child and now I would be raising five boys all alone.

As our priest talked about Mike and life and death I rested my hands on my still flat stomach. Christine was the only other person who knew about this baby. Well, I'm sure Mike knew now but he certainly wouldn't have anything to say about it.

The service ended and we all left the grave site but I couldn't just walk away. I kept looking back and stopping to turn and stare at what was left of my husband. A box.

The boy I had fallen in love with so many years ago was now nothing more than a shell. Finally for the last time that day, with tears coursing down my cheeks I turned away and climbed into the back of my parent's car.

Lo – 36
7 Years Ago

"That's it, we're done." Axle said falling to the ground beside me. Once again we were on the edge of the football field at the high school we graduated from. Only this time the kids on the field were babies compared to us.

"Yup, got our discharge papers," I said nodding solemnly. "A lot's changed since we sat here last time."

"Ain't that the truth brother?" Axle said popping the tab on a can of beer.

"What the fuck man? You just get out of CF and you're going for public drunkenness?"

"Hardly, just celebrating, you can drive me home."

"I got a two bedroom downtown, you movin' in?" I asked, watching the boys on the field again. The coach was different but the yelling was the same.

"Yeah," he sighed and guzzled his beer, then crushed the can. "Nowhere else to go."

"You go see your mom?"

"Yeah, she's a shell of her former self." Axle said bitterly. "Kat's the same, crazy little girl driving her dad nuts but she's doing good I guess, time to move on."

"I guess," I replied nodding. "Now what?"

"I don't know man. Mandated therapy sessions with a doc that's never been overseas and never seen the atrocities of war I guess."

"I guess, and work?"

"I was always a decent mechanic, I can do that I suppose. What about you?"

I shrugged, "What if I opened up a shop of our own? You wanna be head mechanic?"

"Sure, you gonna go back to school?"

"Yeah, I'll take a couple of classes I suppose."

"All right, let's get going, my ass is getting cold. You lead, I'll follow to our new castle."

"Casa de Winters coming up." I smirked at Axle and levered myself off the ground feeling a lot older and wiser than the last time we left this field.

Alana – 36
6 Years Ago

"Dammit Mike!" I screamed at the ceiling of the hospital room.

"Keep pushing, Alana!" Christine said beside me, holding my leg up near my chest.

"Fuck you Christine! I am going to curse Mike all I want!"

"One more push Alana," The doctor said and then I felt my baby slip from my body. Something was wrong though, he wasn't making any sounds. The doctor cleaned out his nose and mouth and laid him on my chest.

"Why isn't he crying?" I asked, wiping all the yuck from his little head.

"Don't worry, he's breathing," the nurse said, taking the baby to weigh him. "His colour is good and he's a good weight, 8 lbs 5 oz. Not all babies cry when they're born."

I didn't not feel placated, I felt condescended to. Did this woman in her first year of nursing think she knew more about childbirth than I did when I just gave birth to my fifth child? Ok, granted I was totally stressed out, I was giving birth to that fifth child with my best friend instead of my husband since said husband was dead, but still.

"What is baby's name?" The annoying nurse asked as she handed him back to me all bundled up and warm.

"Drew Michael," I responded looking down at my very quiet baby. I tickled his cheek and he tried to root my finger so I pulled up my shirt and gave him my breast. Little monster latched on right away with no problems. Maybe a quiet baby is ok . . .

"Take baby!" The doctor suddenly ordered.

"What?" I asked, suddenly feeling weak.

"We can't get the bleeding under control; take the baby and the friend." The nurse hustled Christine out of the room as the doctor called for more help. "Let's get some oxytocin in her . . ."

***

"All right mama, let's get you in the shower and cleaned up." The nurse said as I lifted Drew to my shoulder to burp him. "Other mama can finish with the little man."

"I'm sorry, what?" I demanded looking at this woman.

"We need to get you in the shower and cleaned up so we can get you across the hall to recovery." The nurse said slowly, enunciating each of her words.

"Yeah, I gave birth, I'm not stupid." I said, sarcastically. "I've done this a few times before, in this very hospital."

"Of course," the nurse said with a sickly smile. She gently took Drew from me and gave him to Christine and helped me into the shower then disappeared. I gladly washed the sweat and yuck from my body then quickly got back out and dressed in my pajamas. I wanted my little man back.

When I came out the same nurse was there with a wheelchair and Christine was gathering up my things to take across the hall.

"All right mama one, mama two has baby and we are on the move." The nurse said wheeling the chair rather quickly.

"What is she talking about?" I looked at Christine who giggled down at Drew but shook her head.

"Here we are mama one, let's get you into the bed and you can relax." Nurse Ratchett settled me on the bed and asked if there was anything else I needed. I said no and she quickly wheeled the chair out and was gone.

"What the hell was that about?"

"She thinks we're lesbians." Christine laughed out loud. Drew slept through the loud crack of Christine's voice. I frowned at the baby then realized what Christine had said.

"What? Why would she think we're lesbians?"

"Because I was in the room with you and that's usually the spouse's job."

"Did no one mention to her that my spouse is dead?" I snarked, kind of insulted that the nurse would jump to that conclusion.

"Apparently not," Christine laughed again then handed me Drew. He had started to get fussy but was still not making any sounds. Either way I fed him again and let him sleep then rested myself.

Three days later I was waiting for the doctor to check both Drew and I so we could go home. I was sitting on my bed with my mom, filling out paperwork that needed to be done for government records. The nurse who had checked Drew's hearing earlier in the day came back with the same machine.

"Hi, sorry for this, we just need to redo the test on Drew's ears, won't take a minute." She said smiling.

I smiled back and continued talking to my mom about what I was going to do when everything had settled. I was coming to the realization that I couldn't raise five boys by myself, work a full time job, pay for a house and all the other bills that came with life. It was becoming abundantly clear to me that we needed to sell the house and move down closer to my mom and dad.

Mike's parents had passed away when we were still in university, ironically in a car accident and his sister and I had never been close. As a matter of fact I was pretty sure she hated me, but then she seemed to hate everyone.

The only person it would be hard to leave behind was Christine and she was pushing for us to move. She had seen over the last nine months or so how hard life had been on all of us. She even had offered to buy our house.

The nurse left when she was done with Drew and we waited some more for the doctor to come in and release us. When the doctor finally arrived I was afraid it was so late we would be spending another night in the hospital. I was still sore from giving birth and then having an emergency hysterectomy because the doctor couldn't get the bleeding under control.

"Well Mrs. Martin," She said smiling but I could tell there was something else going on. "You are free to go home, the discharge papers are done but I would like you to bring Drew back to see the audiologist first thing Monday morning."

"Why?" I asked, confused.

"Well, Drew failed the routine hearing test we did both times. It's one thing to fail once or for us to not get a clear reading but for a baby to clearly fail the test twice gives us reason to pause."

The doctor was very serious but still sounded optimistic.

"So you're saying Drew might be deaf?" I asked, stupefied.

"Yes, it looks that way." The doctor said nodding.

"Well hell," I said, sharing a look of abject fear with my mother.

Lo – 38

5 years ago

I was sitting at the kitchen table in the apartment I shared with my best friend Axle when he came slamming in.

As I watched, Axle slammed the front door closed, threw his jacket on the floor and stomped into the kitchen. He whipped open the fridge and grabbed two beers, handing me one. He twisted the top off of his and chugged it then grabbed another one and sat opposite me.

"Rough day?" I asked as he sat sullenly.

He scoffed at me, "I don't know if this therapy shit is working." We tipped our bottles up and I waited patiently for him to continue. "I feel worse now than when I went in this afternoon. Isn't the point of counselling to help you feel better about the shit we saw in the Sand Box?"

"Yup," I replied and waited some more. Axle needed to vent and I was good with letting him. Every evening he came home from a counselling session was the same, both for him and for me.

"I think I need to get the fuck out of here."

"And go where?"

"Far, far away. I talked to Kat today. Her dad is riding her case again; my mom is drinking like a fish and possibly dating someone else." Axle said, peeling the label on his bottle, talking about his mom, step-dad and half-sister. "Fuck Lo, I don't know what to do."

"Maybe you're right," I said finishing my beer. "I have one more exam this week and I'm done all this business marketing shit. Maybe we do need to get the hell outta Dodge."

"But like you said, and go where?"

"Like you said, far, far away, how far can we go and stay in the country?"

"Yukon?"

"Think warmer, brother," I said, tipping my head back to look at the ceiling. "I've been looking into a few things. What would you say to moving to Kamloops?"

"Where?" He demanded, his forehead creasing.

"Kamloops, southern BC. Even when it is winter it's not super cold, and there's minimal snow fall. I looked into opening businesses there and I think it looks promising."

"That's great, so now you've got something to move forward with, what am I gonna do there?"

"Well, I was thinking of starting an MC."

"A what?" He demanded.

"MC, motorcycle club, but not like the typical drug and gun running, flesh peddling money laundering kind of MC. I'm thinking everything is above board and legal, but it's about the brotherhood. When we came home two years ago what did we miss most?"

"The family, knowing if I turned around there would be twenty brothers who had my six, on the battlefield and off. I hate to say it, but I miss the structure and the schedule. I even kind of miss being told what to do."

"How many other guys fresh out of the forces feel the same way?" I asked getting up to get us each another beer.

"All of them?" Axle answered, accepting the bottle and twisting the top off, tossing it into the sink.

"Well, this is what I've been talking to the counsellor about. I even went down to the Legion and talked to some of the older vets there. They didn't care so much about the bikes, but they liked the idea of having something to come home to. We can even offer counselling and rehab stuff."

"You want us to counsel other vets?" Axle asked skeptically.

I snorted and shook my head, "No fucker, we wouldn't do it; we'd just make sure it was easily available."

"Huh." Was Axle's answer but I could tell he was thinking seriously about it. "What else?"

"You weren't the only one that had a shit day. Fucking boss is a prick and I'm the only one who knows how to change the fucking oil on the older model cars. We can open a garage for custom work and repair on bikes, can do cars, too. There's a hobby farm for sale just outside of Kamloops and on one end of the property is a good size shop. The farm has a house, barn and a few acres. We can open a construction company, too. You think Tank would go with us?"

"Fuck yeah. Tank hates it here, he only stayed here instead of going home to Alberta 'cause his parents had died and he had no one to go home to."

"Well, you were the only person keeping me here." I said watching Axle. "My parents are long gone, I've got no siblings. I came home here because you were here and I know what Ontario's about but I'm not feelin' it. There's nothing here for either of us."

We sat quietly for a few minutes, each lost in our own thoughts staring off into space. It was a big leap of faith but we were each at the end of our ropes. We had to do something to really move on from the CAF. Maybe this was it.

"Fuck, let's do it." Axle said tipping his bottle back and finishing his beer.

Alana
Present Day

"Hey baby, you're a million miles away, what are you thinking about?" I looked up to see Lo leaning against the door frame of my bedroom in the ranch house.

"Just remembering," I said, shrugging.

"Mike?" I just shrugged, not really wanting to discuss my late husband with my future one. "It's ok baby, you had a life before me and it was important. I don't expect you to forget everything that came before, and what came before was pretty amazing."

"I know, I just can't help thinking you're taking on more than you should have to." I said shaking my head. "I can't even give you kids of your own."

"You know Alana, I never in my life ever thought I would have kids at all."

"Yeah, but all of your friends are having kids now."

"So what? You think I'm not ok with the youngest kid in our house being seven and relatively self-sufficient? Axle is the same age as me and he has a new baby. You think he's getting nearly as much sleep as I am?"

"You're missing the point." I said, getting angry. "You're being obtuse on purpose."

"If I am so what? I don't know what I'm missing and I'm ok with that so why aren't you?"

"Because I do know what you're missing and it's spectacular!" I yelled at him.

"I have no doubt that it is, and I am so happy that I could experience that with someone who could see how spectacular that is, I am not nor would I ever be that man. Even if you were able to have more kids I have never ever wanted to have kids."

"Kids, or kids of your own?" I asked whirling away from him.

"Well since you're bringing six kids to this marriage then I guess I'll have to settle for that won't I? You're kind of a package deal." I sighed heavily and stared out the window. "Look, you are determined to make an issue of this. I am telling you right now I love you and I want to marry you. Not some fictional future kids we could have had, you. I love you. I love your kids and will love them like they are mine but I am happy with that. I am content, satisfied. I don't know how else to say it so you'll understand. You let me know if that's enough for you. I guess you've got a week to decide, hopefully I'll see you at the end of the aisle at the church."

He turned and left the room as tears flowed freely down my cheeks. What was I doing? I had never imagined that I would get married again, or that I would be in a position to. I had always thought and dreamed that Mike and I grew old together and had grandkids and great grandkids and we would live happily ever after.

But, here I was, in love with a man who wasn't Mike, who had swooped into my life and changed everything. I had been happy mostly with my kids and my job and living close to my parents.

I missed Mike and I missed having a man to hold at night. Lo had given that back to me and he had given me so much in the last year. What did I give him? Six kids, lots of baggage and my own neurosis. And yet he said he loved me.

He must have stopped to talk to the kids downstairs because he was only just now leaving the house. He looked up at my bedroom window and stared at me for a minute, then turned and got on his bike and roared away.

"Mom?" Nate asked, standing in the doorway.

"Yeah sweetheart?" I replied, wiping the tears from my face.

"What's going on?"

"Oh, just me being crazy," I sniffed and turned to my oldest son. He looked so much like his dad.

"Lo loves you."

"I know," I chuckled wetly.

"Like he loves you like dad did, maybe more."

I laughed at that, "Oh yeah?"

"Don't do that."

"Don't do what, Nate?"

"Don't assume that because I'm sixteen I don't know what love is or what it looks like. I'm young, not stupid. Lo loves you."

"I know and I love him but I just don't know if I'm enough for him."

"Why not?" Nate demanded crossing his arms over his chest.

"When Drew was born I had to have an emergency hysterectomy, I can't have any more kids."

"So, does Lo care about that?"

"He says no, but Axle's having kids and so is Hammer, Seether is trying with Pixie. I don't want him to be the odd man out. I don't want him to look at us a few months or years down the road and wish for more."

"Why would he do that? He's said over and over he never wanted kids of his own, that he's always been happy without kids."

"Yeah, but he has no siblings, who's going to pass on the Winters name? Isn't that important to men?"

"I'm sure he has cousins to do that, not to mention there are probably hundreds of thousands of men in the world with the last name Winters."

"Nate, Lo should have kids, if for no other reason than to pass on his amazing DNA."

"Mom, that's the dumbest thing I've ever heard." Nate said, shaking his head as he walked out the door. "We will always be beside you and support you no matter what, but we can't give you everything you need. If you let Lo go now you will forever regret it and be unhappy."

Lo

"Hey Ax, what's up?" I asked as I walked into my office to find my VP lying on my couch.

"Just catching up," he mumbled from under his hat.

"On what?"

"Sleep man, babies don't sleep at night." He muttered just as Hammer stumbled into the room.

"True dat," Hammer rumbled dropping into a chair and tipping his head back with his mouth open and his eyes closed.

"And Alana thinks I want this?" I snorted at them as I shook my head.

"Why the hell would she think that?" Hammer demanded lifting his head up.

"Why the hell would who think what?" Seether asked as he shoved Axle's feet off the couch so he could sit down.

"Alana thinks Lo wants a baby." Axle said grumpily as he shifted to sit properly on the couch.

"Is she confused? I want a baby, with Pixie. Lo has never wanted a baby." Seether said looking back and forth between the guys. This wasn't new, these three could sit in a room with someone and talk around them like they didn't even exist and completely figure out all the world's ills. "You don't want a baby do you?"

"No, I don't want a baby." I answered Seether.

"Did you tell her that?"

"Yes, I told her that."

"Huh," he said his brow wrinkling.

"Don't get me wrong man, I love Imogen and I wouldn't give her up for the world but I miss sleeping." Axle said, settling his hat on his head.

"Ditto," Hammer said nodding and rubbing his eyes at the same time. "You think you've got it bad, you've only got one, I've got three. Fuck we don't ever sleep. If it wasn't for Pixie Kat really would never sleep."

"And she thinks I want this."

"Don't get me wrong man," Hammer said shaking his head now, "Babies are amazing. Seeing both me and Kat in those three little faces, watching them grow and change and learn is the most amazing thing in the world. It's something I never thought I would want but that doesn't mean that everyone wants or needs that."

"It also doesn't mean that everyone should want or need that." Axle said, agreeing with Hammer.

"Yeah well, Alana's on the verge of calling off the wedding because she thinks she has nothing to give me. She thinks she has nothing to bring to this marriage."

"Fuck, she's as bad as Pixie." Seether muttered. "You guys remember when we bought the house? She freaked because she wasn't contributing financially. It took a whole hell of a lot of begging on my part and a serious talk from Kat, to get her to agree."

"Maybe Kat should go talk to Alana then." I said shaking my head.

"I just dropped her and the babies over there." Hammer said, shrugging.

"Pixie's over there right now, too." Seether said nodding.

"I wouldn't be surprised if Brooke joined them in the next five minutes." Axle muttered, already falling asleep again.

Alana

"Hey, come down stairs," Pixie said standing in the doorway of my room. "Kat's downstairs and she doesn't want to carry all the babies up here. Brooke's on her way over, too."

"Oh great," I mumbled. "Did Lo send you all over?"

"Uh, no," Pixie said confused. "Not me anyway, Kat said she wanted to come and visit and since I was there and Hammer and Aiden had to come here anyway I just came along. What's going on, you ok?"

"No I am not ok, but I'm sure I'm going to have to tell everyone so I might as well come down and tell everyone at once."

"You're scaring me," Pixie said as she followed me down the stairs.

"Oh good, Brooke is here, I can say this once and you can all yell and not change my mind and we can move on."

"What the heck?" Brooke demanded on a whisper.

"I don't feel like I'm bringing anything to this marriage with Lo. I feel like I'm bringing a lot of baggage that he doesn't need and I feel like I can't even give him a child of his own to carry on his lineage or whatever."

"Alana that's the dumbest thing I've ever heard." Kat said, shaking her head. "Lo doesn't want a baby, his or anyone else's."

"Axle tells me all the time he's too old for this shit," Brooke said sitting on the couch with Imogen. "Trust me, if Lo says he doesn't want a baby then he doesn't want a baby."

"Are you sure you're not confusing him with Aiden?" Pixie asked, looking at me like I was crazy.

"You guys don't get it." I said shaking my head. "I had that, what you have now, with Mike and it was great and wonderful. And then I had Drew and I can't have kids anymore. Enter Lo who has never experienced childbirth and raising kids and infants and all the rest of it and he thinks he doesn't want any kids of his own. He doesn't know what he's missing, but I do."

"Is this a big deal because we're all having babies?" Brooke asked skeptically.

"Yes and no." I said slumping in Lo's chair. "I just think this is something he's going to want one day and I can't give it to him."

"Uh, I still think you're crazy." Pixie said, shaking her head. "Lo is what, forty-three, forty-four? I think by now he knows his own mind."

"He has no experience to draw from." I said shaking my head.

"I'll tell you what; I'll find a reason to get Lo to stay at our place for a couple of nights. Then he'll have experience to draw from and know for a fact that he doesn't want kids."

"That's not the same and you know it." I snarked at Brooke, "That's just exposing him to the hard parts, not the fun parts."

"Um, I think you get to do the fun parts without worrying about the hard parts." Kat smirked at me and bopped her eyebrows.

"You guys aren't taking this seriously." I wailed at them just getting more upset.

"Kat, tell her what you told me when I was upset about Aiden buying a house." Pixie said pointing at me.

"I told her if she wanted to contribute financially then get a job and do it." Kat said, shrugging.

"Well it's not like that applies, it's not like I can go out and get a new uterus and get pregnant." I humphed.

"True," Kat said shrugging, "But as close as we all are do you really think that Lo isn't experiencing our pregnancies right along with our men? I mean no he's not the one going out at all hours for cravings and he's not the one in the delivery room, but I'm pretty sure Sam told me once he had to help deliver a baby in the forces. I bet Axle and Lo had to do the same at least once, they were in longer than Sam was."

"That's true," Brooke said nodding, "When I was giving birth David said something about remembering this whole thing being a lot louder. When I asked him what he meant he said the last time he was in a birthing room of any kind the woman giving birth was screaming at the top of her lungs. I highly doubt David was involved in something like that and Lo wasn't right there with him."

"I'm sure that Lo has held a newborn fresh out of its mama." Pixie said shrugging her shoulders like that made all the sense in the world.

"Ok, this is slightly helpful," I muttered at them caustically.

"And really, what man wants to be involved in three am feedings? Like really, even with three babies Sam brings me one then falls asleep again, I do the rest." Kat said, shrugging. "Of course he gets up early with them and lets me sleep in. Is that what you think Lo is missing out on?"

"No . . . I don't know, I just feel like he's going to regret us some time down the road."

"I reiterate; that is the dumbest thing I have ever heard." Kat said, shaking her head. "In the last year have you ever known Lo to regret anything?"

"No, but –"

"No buts, Lo doesn't make rash decisions, ever." Brooke said forcefully. "That's Axle's job. Lo thinks things to death and then he makes a decision and he sticks to it. He thought about you and he made his decision and he loves you. He's not going to regret you, ever."

"You didn't assume Mike would regret you." Pixie pointed out.

"That's because Mike and I did everything together from the beginning."

"You and Mike didn't raise a deaf boy from the beginning; you and Mike didn't move your whole family to a new province together from the beginning. You and Mike did a lot together from the beginning, it's true but there's been a lot that Mike hasn't been here for. Now you can do other stuff with Lo together from the beginning, like sending your first kid to college, or your kids dating." Brooke said gently, standing with Imogen in her arms and then placing the baby in mine.

"I think you're thinking this to death and you just need to let go and let God." Kat said, shrugging. "Isn't that what your mom always says?"

Lo

It had been two days since I walked out on Alana and I was seriously regretting it. I had basically given her an ultimatum and I wasn't all that confident that she would choose me. I might be completely fucked. I was ready to get up and go over to the house and beg her to marry me.

And then Axle knocked on the door of my room at the clubhouse.

"Your woman is fucking crazy." He said pushing me out of the way and flopping on my bed.

"What are you talking about?"

"You remember that time we were in Kandahar and we had to deliver that woman's twins?"

"Yeah, hard to forget man,"

"Yeah, I just spent two hours going over that entire day. How you felt, how I felt, how you looked when you held the babies, did you look wistful, did you look jealous of the dad. Holy shit I thought I was going to carve my own eyes out with a fucking spoon."

"I was not wistful and I was not jealous. It was amazing and then I gladly handed each of those babies off to whoever was next to me." I said shaking my head.

"Yeah well, I think I conveyed that quite clearly but she might be crying right now 'cause I yelled at her, sorry."

"Fuck," I tipped my head back and looked at the ceiling, my hands on my hips. "Is it horrible right now that I think her crying alone is teaching her a lesson?"

"What kind of lesson?" Axle asked skeptically.

"The kind of lesson where I could be with her consoling her and helping her feel better but instead I'm here because she thinks I want more than her?"

"Huh," Axle muttered looking up at me. "So you're saying that she's going to realize she can't live without you because you make everything better?"

"Yeah, I think so."

Axle shrugged, "Sure, why not, make her miserable for the next few days so she realizes she can't live without you... or she realizes she's strong enough to get over, around and through anything without a man in her life."

"Shut the fuck up asshole." I muttered and left the room with Axle's laughter ringing in my ears.

"Hey Lo," Nate said from the couch in the main room of the clubhouse. He was sitting there with Chelle and three of his four brothers.

"Hey, what are you guys doing here?"

"Mom's going nuts; we came here to get away from her." Cal shrugged not taking his eyes from the show they were all watching.

"Where's Drew?"

"He turned off his hearing aid, he can't hear her." Jack explained.

"Lucky little bastard," Cal said and the others nodded.

"You guys know I love your mom right?" I asked looking at these five kids sitting on my couch. "You know I don't want any more from her or you guys than her and you guys right?"

"Yeah Lo, we're good." Link said and the rest nodded again.

"What am I going to do about your mother?"

"Pray." They all said at once. That's just fucking awesome.

Alana

I was in the kitchen making breakfast, two more nights until our rehearsal dinner. The boys and Chelle were taking advantage of the summer hours and sleeping in, well all except Drew. He came running in from the back yard and skidded to a stop in front of me. He looked at me for a few minutes and I smiled at him, waiting to see if he was going to talk to me or stare at me.

Are you going to marry Lo? He signed.

I don't know. I want to but I don't know.

You have to, I don't have a dad like my brothers. Lo could be my dad.

You know your dad is the same as your brothers' dad.

Yeah but I didn't know him. I've never had a dad and I want Lo to be my dad.

How would you want Lo to be your dad? I signed, my heart breaking for my little boy. I had no idea he felt this way and he was so little I never thought to ask him.

He could adopt me, Nate said so.

"What's the shrimp talking about?" Nate asked, yawning as he walked into the kitchen.

179

"He said you told him that Lo could adopt him." I replied, not taking my eyes off my youngest son.

"Well, he could, I mean if he wanted to and you were ok with it right?"

"What would make you think of that?" I asked Nate.

"I don't know, Drew asked me once what dad was like and why he had never met him." Nate shrugged.

"What do you think about Lo adopting Drew? Would you guys want Lo to adopt you, too?"

"No," Nate said, shaking his head. "Cal, Jack, Link and I are good, we had dad and he's still dad and always will be. Lo is more like a really cool guy that you marry and we live with and will kind of act like our dad but better. Drew never had that at all, except for grandpa. The rest of us think it's cool if that's what the three of you want."

"Huh," I said looking between my boys. *Drew, do you want Lo to adopt you, would you want his last name and to call him dad?*

Drew looked at me for a minute without saying or signing anything, and then he smiled and nodded and ran from the room.

Lo

Two more nights until our rehearsal dinner; which was actually a family bar-b-que at the clubhouse. According to the kids Alana was spending a lot of time in her room staring wistfully out the window.

She spent a lot of time going through old photo albums of her and Mike and the kids. She also spent a lot of time going through the photo albums of her and the boys after Mike had died.

She didn't know it but I spent a lot of time at night sitting under her bedroom window. I hated being away from her and this was the longest we'd been apart since we met a year ago. I missed her as much as I wanted her to miss me, maybe more.

That's where I was right now; or rather I was sitting on the porch swing that was under her window. I was trying to talk myself out of going up to her room and making love to her. We hadn't made love here in the house while the kids were home but right now I didn't care.

They all knew we had sex, at least Nate and Chelle and probably Cal did. I hated being away from her, I hated it. Nope, wasn't going to convince myself to stay away tonight.

I got up and opened the front door, punched my code into the alarm and quietly ran up the stairs. I tapped on her door then opened it and walked in, closing the door behind me.

"What are – Lo? What are you doing here?" She asked, she was standing beside her bed with her phone in her hand.

I walked over to her and took the phone, putting it on the night stand then took her in my arms and kissed her like I hadn't seen her in weeks, not just days. She responded immediately and re-turned my kiss, her hands fisted in my shirt.

My hands were in her hair and on her back and pushing her shirt up and off and thank God she wasn't wearing a bra.

"Lo –"

"Sh, I've kept myself away from you for three days and I can't take it anymore," I said and pulled my own shirt off over my head then kissed her again, cupping her beautiful breasts in my hands. "I can't stay away from you anymore, I can't live without you."

I kissed her again, running my hands all over her perfect naked skin. God I was starting to feel like a horny teenager, I had to have her. I shoved my hands into her pajama pants and pushed them down her legs.

I couldn't remember the reason she gave me for not wearing underwear to bed but I was sure glad of it now. I kissed and sucked down her stomach until I was kneeling in front of her, my face buried in her pussy.

"Fuck I missed you," I whispered then dragged my tongue from her opening to her clit, sucking it into my mouth. "I missed your taste and your smell and the feel of your skin on mine and the sound of your breathing. Please baby, please don't make me live without you."

I was begging, I was fucking begging her. Just what I swore I wouldn't do but I had to, I had to have her and I would put aside my pride if it meant I would have her. I looked up at her, all the love I felt for her in my eyes.

"Alana –"

"Stop!" She cried panting as she looked down at me, then she crouched and kneeled in front of me. "Stop, Lo, I love you, you don't need to beg, please don't beg. I'm so sorry my actions brought you to that." Tears were flowing down her cheeks as she started sobbing. "I'm so sorry," She whispered over and over again.

"Baby, stop, I love you. You're scared I get it, but listen to me and understand when I tell you, you are the only thing in this world that I want. If all you ever give me for the rest of my life is your love I will be the luckiest son of a bitch in the world. Yes, if it were possible I would love to have a baby with you, I would love to see you pregnant with my child, but that is not possible and I am so happy and in love with you and with our life as it is that I don't need that to love you any more than I already do."

"Lo –" she kissed me softly then rubbed her hands up my chest and into my hair.

I pulled her into my lap then holding her tight I stood and laid her gently on the bed. I stood and undid the button and zipper on my jeans, pushing them down my legs and off as she scooted back on the bed.

I crawled over to her, kissing first her foot, then up the inside of her leg, then across from one hip bone to the other and up again until I reached her throat.

I sucked at the pulse point in her throat as she raked her nails across my back and arched her hips up into me. I lifted from her throat and kissed her mouth, licking my tongue inside just as I thrust my cock into her tight wet channel.

Every thrust of my tongue mimicked the thrust of my cock until I had to pull back to take a breath. I changed my pace, surging quickly into her, twisting my hips to grind against her clit then pulling out slowly only to repeat it, leaving her gasping.

I pulled her knee up to her chest and hooked my arm around her lower leg, opening her to me more and rested my forehead on hers then pumped harder and faster into her. Just as she arched her neck and pushed her head into the bed, clenching me with her pussy muscles I felt the tickle in my lower back and I erupted inside her.

"Fuck baby, Alana I love you so fucking much." I whispered, kissing her, sipping at her lips until I could finally move.

I rolled off of her, bringing her with me to lie on our sides facing each other. She still had tears tracking slowly down her cheeks but I believed now they were happy tears.

"Lo I love you so, so much. I'm so sorry I put you through that." She shook her head then buried her wet face in my throat.

"It's ok, you're mine forever right? We're getting married in two days and we will always be like this together?"

"Yes, tomorrow night we will have our rehearsal dinner, then the next day we will meet at the altar at the church and we will get married. For better or worse for ever and ever, I am never letting you go."

"Get some sleep baby," I said, kissing her forehead. "I'm gonna have to sneak out of here in a few hours and I'm gonna want to have you again."

Alana giggled and snuggled into me, holding me as tight as I was holding her.

Alana
Rehearsal Bar-B-Que

I had realized the other night when Lo had come to my room how ridiculous I was being. I had my phone in my hand to call him when he came into my room. Then to have him beg me just made me feel horrible, even if it did solidify my realization that I was being ridiculous. I had prayed for days and talked to friends and my sister and my mother and every time the answer was you're being ridiculous. I had to agree.

Now we stood in the backyard of the clubhouse with all of our friends and family around us, and I knew for a fact that marrying Lo was the right thing to do. My children loved him and respected him and he loved them. He wanted to have them in his life and he wanted to be a good role model for them. He even became Catholic for us, though I know that he truly believes in our faith.

My brother came up to us and hugged me, eyeing Lo the entire time.

"Don't make me kill you," Ray rumbled at Lo, cracking his knuckles. Lo just smiled at my brother and held out his hand.

Ray looked at the hand extended to him and after a few seconds of debate reached out and shook it.

"Stop it Raymond," my mother said pushing my brother out of the way and shooing him across the yard and following him to make sure he behaved himself. My sister came over to chat and hug and chat some more until one of her kids came screaming out of the clubhouse soaking wet.

"Oh fuck," Lo muttered as Krystal ran after her child.

"Don't worry baby, whatever mess he made I'll clean it up."

"Nah, that's what we've got prospects for." Lo smirked and pointed at one of the younger guys standing beside the door inside. The prospect nodded then disappeared through the door.

Later, after everyone had headed home or to hotels Lo and I sat on the swing on the front porch of the house. It was quiet upstairs and the crickets and frogs were singing out in the field. We sat quietly, snuggled together as Lo pushed the swing gently with one foot.

"It's so peaceful here." I said resting my head on his shoulder.

"Don't get used to it, tomorrow's going to be insane."

"That's true, and on that note I need to get my beauty sleep." I said and kissed him, then left him on the swing.

Alana
Wedding Day

Today was the day. I couldn't believe it was here, that even after the crazy week Lo and I had just had we were getting married today. I sat in front of my mirror while my sister did my makeup and Kat did my hair. I was getting married today, for the second time.

I knew Lo would be waiting for me at the altar and thinking about how handsome he would be in his suit had me twisting my engagement ring. Lo hadn't bought it yet when he'd asked me to marry me but that was ok.

He gave me the ring for Christmas. It was two tear drop shaped diamonds touching at the points with clusters of the kids' birthstones around them. The band was platinum and matched the wedding rings we would exchange later at the church.

"Ok, I think you're ready," my sister said after one last swipe of mascara.

"Yup, I agree," Kat said, stepping back to look at her work. "Where's the dress?"

"It's in the closet." I said pointing to the walk in closet Lo had built when the guys had renovated the house a year ago.

"This really is a spectacular dress," Kat said as she carried it out of the closet. "Sit where you are and we'll lift it over your head."

The dress was something I had designed because I couldn't find anything that I loved. It was a very simple tea length sheath dress in a soft pink satin that complimented my skin tone perfectly. It also had a layer of silver Guipure lace over top.

It was modest but I knew Lo would see the sexiness of it. My shoes were simple pumps that matched the pink of my dress. Brooke was my only bridesmaid and she would be wearing a simple dress of her choosing.

Lo would be wearing a simple gray suit and Axle his grooms-man would be wearing a simple navy suit. Everything was simple and understated. We wanted people to see that while the wedding was wonderful and fun it was the marriage that was important. We were giving each other a covenant, not just a promise.

The boys would all walk me down the aisle and Lo had planned to include them in his vows. What he didn't know was that they too had vows for him. He would be, I hoped, pleasantly surprised.

"Ok, let's get going." My dad said sticking his head in the door of my room. "Sweetheart, you are beautiful."

He hugged me lightly, knowing better than to mess up my hair and makeup. Then we were off to the church. It was Saturday afternoon and only our guests were at the church. It was by far not packed, doing this the second time around I knew I didn't want a crazy over the top ceremony.

When we arrived at the church Kat and Krystal rushed up the aisle to their seats and got settled in. As soon as the priest was notified that I had arrived he came back and started the procession for the mass. The music was beautiful, the guests were beautiful and even my brother was dressed respectfully, I wish though that I could say the same about his date du jour.

Then Brooke was starting down the aisle towards the altar and I could tell by the tilt of her head that she was only looking at Axle who held Imogen in his arms. He was smiling so widely I thought his face would crack. And then it was our turn. Link, Drew and Jack in front and Cal and Nate on either side of me, walked me down the aisle to our future and the rest of our lives.

Lo
Wedding Day

She was beautiful; I mean I knew Alana was beautiful, she'd always been beautiful. The dress she was wearing hugged her curves so perfectly and the way it shimmered in the candle light was hypnotic. Axle snorted and nudged me, reading my mind about the dress.

Shit, pay attention Lo. Alana's boys handed her off to me and then surrounded us at the altar. I didn't know this was their plan and from the look on their mother's face neither did she, but she just smiled at them and winked.

We said our vows to each other and exchanged our rings and then I turned to the boys and Chelle who was sitting in the front row.

"I wanted to tell you guys something," I said, clearing my throat. "I've only been in your lives for a year and in that year I have grown to love you all. You are all smart and funny and full of so much potential. I asked you boys before I asked your mom if you had any problems with me marrying her and Nate, quick as ever said, if you marry her you marry us, we're a package deal so make sure you're up for the challenge."

The congregation laughed at that, most of them knew Nate pretty good.

"After that, I worked hard to prove not just to Alana but to you boys that I could and would be the man you all needed me to be. That effort didn't end today, yes your mom and I are married, just about," I said as the priest cleared his throat, "But now the effort begins in earnest and it will never end. I will forever work hard to be worthy of you all."

Alana and many of the other women had tears in their eyes and Nate had a gleam in his as well. Then he surprised me when he stepped forward with a piece of paper in his hands.

"Lo, we all wrote this, each of us put something in it and this is what we want you to know. Over the last year you have proven to us that you love our mom and respect her for the fantastic person she is. We appreciate that more than you know. You have been a role model and example of how a man should be; with other men, with other women and with the woman he claims to love. We know when you say you love mom and us that it's not a claim but a promise. So, we promise to be the best sons we can be to you, we promise to work hard to make you proud, and we promise to make you question your sanity at least once in a while."

Even through my tears I threw my head back and laughed out loud, and then I gathered all the kids into my arms and hugged them tight. Chelle stepped up to the altar as well and hugged us all.

I turned to Alana but she was watching Drew, the littlest of them all. She gave him a slight nod and I felt him tug on my hand. I frowned slightly then looked down at him, he crooked his finger and motioned for me to get closer so I crouched down in front of him.

Mommy says it's ok if you adopt me. I don't have a dad 'cause he died, will you be my dad?

I think I started crying in earnest after that and I let the tears flow freely as I grabbed this little boy and held him tightly against my chest. I ruffled his hair and kissed his cheek then looked him straight in the eyes.

"It would be my honor to adopt you and give you my name just like your mom. I would be so proud to have you call me dad." I cupped his face in both my hands and kissed his forehead then hugged him again. After that he wouldn't let me go and we finished the ceremony with him in my arms.

It took everyone a few minutes to settle and dry their eyes but when we were all tear free we continued the ceremony.

Alana and I exchanged our rings, each engraved with "forever and always" on the inside and then the priest pronounced us Mr. and Mrs. Logan and Alana Winters. I think after the boys' speech that was my favourite part. She was mine, forever.

Alana

Reception

Our reception was a little more fancy than our rehearsal bar-b-que, but not by much. We had rented a hall that would fit everyone and had hired a band. We got our supper catered and everyone was enjoying their time dancing and laughing and taking pictures.

We decided that instead of having posed wedding pictures we would have family pictures done in a week and have as many candid photos taken at the reception as possible.

Speeches were made and Lo actually thanked Mike for being the amazing father and husband he was before he was taken too soon. Lo had a knack for making people cry. Then it was time for our first dance as husband and wife.

The band started playing the first bars of the first song Lo and I had ever danced to. I couldn't believe he remembered it, but I should have known he would.

Lo
Reception

As I held Alana in my arms and swayed back and forth to Heaven by Bryan Adams I couldn't help but remember the first time we had danced to this song. We had only been seeing each other for a couple of months but I knew even then that I loved her and I wanted to marry her. I knew even then I wanted to spend the rest of my life with her.

I held her close to me now and sang softly along with the words in her ear, thinking about how the words were so perfect for our story.

She hadn't been the only one thinking about the past this last week. I had been thinking about all the hell I'd gone through to get to where I was now, holding the most amazingly perfect woman in my arms.

I really truly was in heaven.

Printed in Great Britain
by Amazon

86191933R20108